Love Takes a Country Road

Janet Hayward Burnham

G.K. Hall & Co. • Chivers Press
Thorndike, Maine USA   Bath, England

This Large Print edition is published by G.K. Hall & Co., USA and by Chivers Press, England.

Published in 1999 in the U.S. by arrangement with Juliet Haywood Burnham.

Published in 1999 in the U.K. by arrangement with the author.

U.S. Softcover   0-7838-8614-4   (Paperback Series Edition)
U.K. Hardcover   0-7540-3828-9   (Chivers Large Print)
U.K. Softcover   0-7540-3829-7   (Camden Large Print)

The text of this Large Print edition is unabridged.
Other aspects of the book may vary from the original edition.

Set in 16 pt. Plantin by Al Chase.

Printed in the United States on permanent paper.

British Library Cataloguing in Publication Data available

Library of Congress Cataloging in Publication Data

Burnham, Janet Hayward.
     Love takes a country road / Janet Hayward Burnham.
       p.   cm.
     Originally published in 1991 under the author's pseudonym:
Jessie Mina Scott.
     ISBN 0-7838-8614-4 (lg. print : sc : alk. paper)
     1. Large type books. I. Title.
[PR6052.U6573L68 1999]
823´.914—dc21
                                                              99-21839

To Reina and Coonish, whose antics enlivened our lives and made this book possible. And to Scott, Mark, Hilary and Kristen, who were owned by so many furry, fluffy, feathered, slithery, lumpy, bumpy four-legged and otherwise critters.

One

She had only let her eyes drift from the road momentarily. When she looked back, there was a black and white animal directly in her path. Elizabeth swerved to the other side of the dirt road, the car sliding sideways in the loose gravel. Suddenly a pick-up loomed in front of her. Elizabeth jammed the steering-wheel in the other direction. Her mother's old station-wagon swayed violently, threatening to tip. It didn't come to a stop until it hit the ditch. Elizabeth let out a ragged sigh of relief. Luckily, she was wearing a seat-belt. Since the children had been born, she had taken to wearing a seat-belt. It was automatic now. And the few times she did forget, Josh or Trudy were certain to remind her. The first thing she thought, as the old car shuddered and stood still, was thank goodness the children weren't with me.

The driver of the pick-up had stopped and was out of his vehicle and heading her way. Elizabeth braced herself for the tirade he was surely going to deliver. He had, she told herself, every reason to be angry.

She took a deep breath, unhitched her seat-belt with shaking hands and opened the door of the station-wagon. She would at least take her medicine eye to eye. As she stood up, she was surprised to find her knees didn't want to co-operate. She grabbed the car door for support and felt a strong hand catch her elbow.

'Are you all right?' The voice was gentle, kindly. Elizabeth couldn't help but notice it held no hint of the anger she had expected.

'I . . . I think so,' she stammered. 'I guess I'm a little shook up.'

'I should think so,' he answered. 'You had quite a wild ride there for a few minutes.' She looked up into brown eyes that were regarding her solicitously. 'Here,' he continued, 'lean against the car until you recover your sea legs.'

Elizabeth leaned back against the old red station-wagon and he released her elbow. She noted that he smelled of woodsmoke and a musky aftershave.

Elizabeth shut her eyes and tried to collect her thoughts. What was she doing in Vermont anyhow? And what was she doing thinking about aftershave, when she had almost had a serious accident? Her eyes flew open. 'Are *you* all right?' she asked, and wondered how she could have almost forgotten to ask the most obvious question.

'I'm fine,' he almost smiled. 'Just momentarily surprised, that's all.'

"Thank goodness.' She breathed a sigh of relief. 'I don't usually drive on the wrong side of the road,' she began to explain.

He didn't say anything, but his thick black brows shot up in question, like ravens rising.

'There was an animal in the road,' she went on, shaking her head. 'I didn't want to hit it.'

He had taken out his pipe and was carefully filling it from an old leather pouch of tobacco. 'Black and white?' He was nodding his head.

'Yes, but how did you know?'

He lit his pipe and the aroma of the smoke curled around a memory in Elizabeth's mind. Grandfather! Her grandfather had smoked that same tobacco. Dear sweet grandfather.

'I've almost hit that little stinker myself,' he grinned at her. 'It's a skunk. She lives somewhere close by and this is a favourite road crossing for her.'

'A skunk!' Elizabeth could just imagine returning her mother's car reeking of skunk.

'Skunks are notoriously poor at watching out for cars . . . or for anything else, for that matter,' he continued. 'They seem to think that everything that moves will watch out for them. Which is pretty much true, except in the case of cars. Nobody's been able to yet convince a skunk that cars have no sense of smell.' He grinned around his pipe. 'One of these days she'll be a flat skunk.'

'Well,' Elizabeth grinned in return, 'I'm glad I didn't flatten her.'

Elizabeth was amazed to see him take one last puff on his pipe and put it in the pocket of his flannel shirt. She wondered why he didn't set himself on fire. 'Too bad she didn't do the same for you,' he said.

Elizabeth frowned. She was still keeping an eye on the pipe pocket, expecting to see it burst into flames at any minute. 'What?'

'You've got a flat right front tyre,' he answered, walking around to the front of the station-wagon and shaking his head.

Elizabeth hurried around to the front of the car. Sure enough, the tyre in the ditch was completely flat. 'Oh hell and damnation!' she fumed.

The pipe smoker, whoever he was, was down on one knee peering under the car. 'And you've got a good sized hole in your radiator. I'm afraid your good deed has put your good old Bessie here out of commission for a while.' He patted the front of the station-wagon and stood up.

Elizabeth threw up her hands in despair. 'I knew I never should have come! I knew it! I told them it was a bad idea! Why I ever let myself get talked into these things, I'll never know!' Elizabeth paced back and forth in the gravel road. 'I should be back in New York right now, studying, or taking the children to the park. But no, I have to be here in Vermont with a car wrecked by a skunk, talking to a total stranger!'

The pipe smoker had taken out his pipe again. He began calmly knocking out the old tobacco against the heel of his boot. Elizabeth couldn't tell if he was listening or not. For some reason that made her all the angrier. She glared in his direction and continued — 'Here I am, all grown up with two kids of my own, and I still think I have to do what my mother and father suggest. "Go to Vermont, Elizabeth. Go see your inheritance, Elizabeth. Check out Uncle Abner's house," they said. "It will be good for you to get

10

away!" Good? I ask you, is this good?' She stopped and watched him light his pipe. 'Well, don't you ever say anything?' she demanded.

He took a few puffs. 'Was I supposed to?'

He had his teeth clamped down tight on the stem of his pipe, so she couldn't tell if he was grinning or not, but he couldn't hide the amusement in his eyes.

'I . . . yes . . . no, I don't know,' she answered miserably.

'Could I offer you a ride somewhere, Elizabeth?' he asked calmly.

'How did you know my name?' she frowned.

'You said it . . . twice in fact,' he answered, in a reasonable tone that made her want to scream.

She was acting irrationally. She knew it and she didn't care. Well, maybe she did care a little. It was her worst fault. Whenever a situation got out of control, she had to let off steam. Her husband Ted had always called it 'Elizabeth's Blow-off'. She had worked hard to control it. It wasn't good for the children to learn to handle frustrations like that, he had said. And she had agreed. But it was hard. Anyway, the children weren't here . . . and she didn't care. What did it matter? Ted was dead and gone. She nervously twisted her wedding-ring.

'Could I offer you a ride somewhere?' the pipe smoker asked again.

'I can't impose on you, Mr . . . ?'

'Stannard,' he answered. 'Gare Stannard.'

'Thank you, Gare Stannard.' She smiled her

smileless smile. How many times had Josh told her, 'Your mouth is smiling, Mommy, but you aren't.'

'I appreciate your offer, Mr Stannard,' she continued, 'but this is my problem.'

'Suit yourself,' he replied, regarding her with an unreadable expression.

'I know you must at the very least think I'm ungrateful,' she went on. 'I mean, I did almost cause an accident. And you've been very kind. Could I call a cab?' She tried to smile a kindly smile, but it didn't feel quite right.

'I suppose you could,' he answered, 'but I doubt that one would hear you from here.' He had his pipe tight in his teeth, but his eyes were smiling way out to the corners.

'You know what I mean,' Elizabeth retorted angrily. She couldn't stand being laughed at. 'Stop laughing at me!'

'I didn't realize that I was,' he answered evenly.

'Hurumpt!' said Elizabeth. She went over and kicked at the good left front tyre.

'Look,' he said finally. 'You can't get much of anywhere from here . . . without a lot of walking. Let me give you a lift to a phone, then you can call whomever you please. Call a cab, or call a garage, or call your husband. I promise I won't attack you, if that's what you're worried about.'

She turned around and regarded him thoughtfully. It had never entered her mind to be afraid of him. He was handsome in an outdoorsey sort of way. He was kind and considerate. What was wrong with her anyway? In another situation, in another place, she might have looked at him very differently. Before she had gathered her thoughts enough to answer him he continued — 'After all, it's the least you can do for me after almost running me off the road and all.'

She had to smile at that. 'That doesn't make any sense at all, you know.'

'I know,' he answered. 'But it's been my observation that very little in this life makes a whole lot of sense. You just have to go along and make the best of whatever life hands you.'

'And smile?'

'Yes,' he answered, 'that too — it helps.'

Elizabeth climbed into the pick-up a little reluctantly. She didn't like the thought of leaving her car on a deserted country road, but she had no other choice.

They rode along in silence for a while. Elizabeth glanced over at Stannard's hands on the steering-wheel. He had big, hardworking hands. She searched her mind for the right word to describe them. Competent, that was it. He had competent hands, so unlike Ted's. Ted's had been long, narrow, artistic hands with carefully manicured nails. Everything about Ted had been carefully manicured, cultivated. Everything done just precisely, correctly. Even his love-making. Elizabeth lovingly patted the memory in her mind. Then a strange thought crept in. What would it be like to have

Stannard's competent hands on her body? What sort of lover was he? She shook her head to dislodge such a disloyal thought. 'No,' she said aloud.

'Excuse me?' Stannard glanced over at her.

'Nothing,' said Elizabeth. 'I was just thinking out loud.'

'Oh,' said Stannard. He cleared his throat. 'A while ago you mentioned an Uncle Abner. You weren't by any chance speaking of Abner Hollins, were you?'

She was silently thankful that he hadn't said 'a while ago during your babbling outburst', or something like that. He was tactful, if nothing else. 'Yes,' she answered, 'Abner Hollins. Did you know him?'

'Knew him well,' Stannard nodded.

'I didn't know him at all,' she offered. 'He was my husband's relative.'

'That's too bad,' Stannard smiled. 'He was well worth knowing. I don't recall Abner ever mentioning any relatives. I thought he was alone in the world.'

'My husband Ted was a distant relative. Abner was his great-uncle, I believe. Anyway, Ted only saw Uncle Abner once, when he was a little boy. There was some sort of family animosity there. Someone eternally mad at someone else. Sad.'

'Those things always are,' Stannard agreed. 'Abner was a fine old fellow. I think you would have liked him.'

Elizabeth wondered how Stannard could make that judgement. He might have known Uncle Abner, but he certainly didn't know anything about her . . . except that she lost her mind in tense situations, she thought unhappily.

'Abner knew all the country ways of doing things,' Stannard continued — 'where to catch the biggest fish — planting by the moon — what wild plants made good medicine.'

Elizabeth thought of Ted. Ted and his city ways. Ted who liked his country tame and evenly planted in the park. Ted who thought camping out was akin to hanging by the thumbs. Ted wouldn't have cared to know or learn Uncle Abner's country ways, but she didn't say so.

'Yes sir,' Stannard continued, 'a young boy could have learned a lot from Abner Hollins.'

And that made her think of her Josh. Joshua who did love the country. Of course he was only seven. Joshua, who had begged to come with her. And Joshua, who had been some of the reason she had decided to at least look at Uncle Abner's property before she sold it.

Stannard turned up a long drive that led to a log cabin nestled into the corner of a hill.

'Nice-looking place,' Elizabeth remarked. 'Do they have a phone?'

'Thank you,' said Stannard. 'And yes, I have a phone.'

'Your place?'

'My place,' he answered.

The interior of the cabin looked just as Elizabeth imagined it should. The furniture was rustic and comfortable. Colourful Navajo rugs hung over the balcony railings and made bright spots of colour on the highly polished hardwood floors. But best of all was the fieldstone fireplace that rose two storeys in the cathedral-ceilinged living-room. Elizabeth could just imagine sitting in front of a roaring fire while the wind and snow whirled around outside on a cold winter's night. She could imagine herself being warm and toasty next to that fire. 'No,' she said aloud to disperse the thought.

'What did you say?' Stannard asked.

'Nothing,' she blushed.

'Do you talk to yourself a lot?' He grinned at her.

'No . . . yes,' she sighed. 'I suppose I do.'

'Don't worry.' He laughed good-naturedly. 'I'm afraid I do the same thing. Tell you what. I won't tell on you if you won't tell on me.' He winked.

Elizabeth felt a rush of liking for Stannard. It was refreshing to find someone who could so easily laugh at himself.

'Where do you keep your phone?' she changed the subject. She decided that she had better get down to business and stop wool-gathering in dangerous territory. She had no desire to make a boyfriend, or even a friend for that matter, out of a nice man in Vermont.

'Over there beside the couch.' Stannard pointed to the tweedy couch pulled up before the massive fireplace. 'Help yourself. I'll be right back.' He headed upstairs two at a time, to where Elizabeth supposed the bedrooms must be. She wondered what they looked like. Would there be a woman's wardrobe hanging in his closet too? Was he married? He wasn't wearing a ring, she had noted that much. But surely there must be at least a girlfriend in his life. Probably several. 'Excuse me,' she called after his retreating back, 'could you recommend a garage?'

He came back and leaned over the balcony railing. 'I'd call Tommy's Garage in Bridgeton if I were you. Tell him you're a friend of mine. He's a whiz of a mechanic and I think his prices are fair.'

Elizabeth checked the directory and dialled Tommy's Garage and idly began to wonder about Stannard again. Stop this, Elizabeth, she told herself severely. Even if he has a harem, it's none of your business.

Two

Tommy of Tommy's Garage finally answered the phone. Elizabeth told him her car's problems and asked how long he thought it would take to repair. He cheerfully told her he would have to look at the damage first before he could estimate how much time he'd need to repair it. 'And,' he continued — 'I have to come and get it before I can look at it. And since I'm all alone here today, I can't come and get it until I close.'

'When would that be?' Elizabeth inquired.

'After six,' Tommy replied in the same cheery tone.

'After six!' Elizabeth protested loudly. 'You don't understand. I need the car right away. I'm from New York and I only came up for the day. I must have it right away.'

There was a chuckle on the other end of the line. 'Old Gare giving you a hard time, is he?'

'What?'

'You did say you were a friend of Gare Stannard's, right?'

'No . . . I mean yes . . . in a way.' Elizabeth fumbled for words. She really didn't think it was necessary to explain to the garage mechanic how she happened to know Gare Stannard. He was supposed to fix her car, not pry into her personal life for heaven's sake.

Tommy was still enjoying his end of the conversation. 'I'll have to speak to the old boy . . . tsk, tsk, tsk! He shouldn't go around settin' ladies' tail-feathers on fire!'

Elizabeth was just about to give Tommy a piece of her mind when Stannard came back down the stairs pulling on a handknit sweater.

'Just a minute,' Elizabeth told Tommy. Then to Stannard she said, 'I'm having some difficulty with your friend Tommy. He seems to be more interested in why you set my tail-feathers on fire, as he puts it, than in fixing my car!'

Stannard chuckled. 'I forgot to tell you he's a character, harmless . . . but a character. Here, let me talk to him.'

Elizabeth handed him the phone.

'Hello, Tommy, this is Gare. What's the story?' Stannard listened, chuckled a few more times, then said, 'Fine,' and hung up.

'Well?' asked Elizabeth.

'Tomorrow at the earliest,' he answered.

'Tomorrow!' squeaked Elizabeth. 'I can't possibly wait until tomorrow!'

'I'm afraid you'll have to,' Stannard replied evenly. 'This isn't downtown Big City. Things are a little slower paced here. Though I doubt you'd get any quicker service anywhere actually. You can't slap it back together with sealing-wax and bubble-gum, you know.'

'But where will I stay? I can't stay here,' she added quickly. She was beginning to think she had walked into a neatly planned trap. Poor little city girl with broken car, friendly neighbourhood mechanic cooperates, and Gare Stannard has female house-guest to play games with over-night.

'I wouldn't dream of asking you,' Stannard replied calmly.

'Could you take me to a motel?' she asked stiffly.

'I could, but the nearest one is twenty miles from here. It would be awfully inconvenient for you. You mentioned an inheritance and Uncle Abner's house in almost the same breath a while ago; am I right in assuming that Uncle Abner's place is the inheritance?'

She pursed her lips and nodded. She didn't much like giving information about herself to anyone. But then, that was what she got for making a babbling fool of herself. It was her own fault. No telling what information might fall from her lips when her dander was up.

'Well then,' he smiled coolly, 'that settles it. You can stay at Uncle Abner's.' He looked at her worried face. 'You'll like it. It's just down the road. We'll stop and get your duds from your car and I'll even throw in some peanut butter and jelly so you won't starve to death.'

Elizabeth reluctantly followed Stannard out to the pick-up. How quickly, she reflected, the power to decide one's own fate can be yanked away.

They rode in silence for a while. Elizabeth stole several sidelong glances at Stannard. Finally she asked, 'What sort of work do you do?'

'Game warden,' he answered, not looking at her.

'I've never met a game warden before, what does a game warden do?'

'Game and wildlife management.'

'What does that entail?'

'It's our job to protect the wild animals in the state; to be sure that the deer herd isn't hunted to extinction, for instance. We're the police force that stands between all the wild animals and the indiscriminate killing that mankind seems prone to,' he finished with some heat. It was obviously a subject he had very strong feelings about.

'Do you tramp around in the woods looking for hunters and counting deer?'

'Sometimes, but it's not usually so hit-and-miss as you might think. Usually we will have a pretty good idea just where to look for hunters. We know our areas, we know where the deer congregate, we know where a hunter is most likely to set up shop. And after a while, we usually know just which hunters are likely to be taking deer illegally.'

'Sounds like a lot of detective work.'

'It is. We're trained by the State Police and have the same powers to arrest and carry firearms.'

'You like it?'

'Very much. I love the wilderness. I hate to see any of it destroyed. It's a constant battle. There's a lot of development going on in the state right now. Maybe some of it is necessary.

But a lot of it is the tragic spoiling of wild areas and of all the wild inhabitants that call that area home.' He punctuated the end of his sentence with a solid thunk on the steering-wheel with the palm of his hand.

Elizabeth looked out of the window at the green landscape rolling by. It wasn't just a pretty postcard, always there to be admired. Evidently, the scenic beauty of Vermont didn't just happen to stay this way without a lot of thought and work. She hadn't really thought about it before. Wild things were just wild things . . . they happened beyond the hand of man. But no, she could now see that they happened because the hand of man was restrained. Interesting.

They stopped at Elizabeth's car just long enough for her to pick up the little flight-bag she had brought along just in case.

A little further down the road Stannard said, 'Here we are.' He pulled into the grassy drive that led to an old Cape Cod that seemed to have grown out of a rise of land that sat back from the road.

'Uncle Abner's?'

'Handsome place, isn't it,' he nodded.

Elizabeth had to admit that Uncle Abner's house was charming. It was badly in need of paint, but she could readily see that a little attention would turn it into a gem. Dollar signs popped into her head, as she calculated what she could get for it. Maybe it would even be enough to see her through law school with something left over for the children's education if she was very very careful.

The late afternoon sun was slanting through the grand old maples in the front yard. A swing hung from one of the mighty branches. 'I thought you said Uncle Abner was alone in the world.'

'He was,' Stannard answered. 'Or at least I thought he was until you came along.'

'Then why the swing?'

'Visiting fireman,' he smiled. He had a marvellous smile that lit up his whole face, like the sun breaking over the mountains. 'Though you don't have to be a child to enjoy a swing,' he added. 'You should give it a try. It might loosen you up a bit.'

Elizabeth bristled. 'Loosen me up? And just how do I need loosening up?'

'Oh,' he spoke slowly and offhandedly, 'you're in such a hurry to get going — get your car back and all. I just thought you might like to simmer down some and enjoy the countryside. No need to get riled up. I meant no offence.'

'I've been simmered down enough for one day, thank you.' Then thinking that that sounded harsher than she had intended, she added, 'No offence taken. It's just that my responsibilities are back in New York. Being forced to stay here makes me nervous, that's all.'

'You mean your children?'

'Yes, my children . . . and everything else.' She felt almost like crying.

Evidently Stannard read her mind, he changed the subject. He began pointing out different sorts of flowers as they drove in the yard. 'In late April that south-facing hill is a carpet of daffodils. And of course this big bruiser here,' he was pointing to a huge green-leaved bush next to the side door, 'is one of Vermont's famous lilacs. In May the smell of lilac drifts all through the house.'

She was watching his face as he spoke. There was a quietness about it. No, quietness wasn't quite the right word. A peacefulness maybe, as though he had most of his life under control, as though he was at peace with his world. She didn't think she'd ever be able to say that about herself. Being a widow with two young children, and a profession choice that wouldn't be hers until several more years of study, being at peace in her world seemed a long way off.

Stannard showed her around the house — Uncle Abner's house — her inherited house. It was sparsely furnished, clean, almost untouched by the twentieth century. The paint had been scrubbed so often that it was almost non-existent on the woodwork. The late slanting sun made puddles of gold on the bare, wide, board floors. 'Lovely old pine,' said Stannard, noting the direction of her gaze. 'A solid old house,' he continued, 'built by Abner's great-grandfather . . . but maybe you knew that?'

'No,' she shook her head.

'Today there aren't many people who've lived

all their lives in the same house.'

'Abner was born here?'

'Yep, right here,' Stannard opened the door into a small room off the kitchen. 'The borning room it was called. Right off the kitchen so it'd be warm from the kitchen fire. In the old days they always kept a fire going in the kitchen.'

Elizabeth peeked into the little room. It had a few old crocks and shelves of what looked like home-made jam.

She brushed by Stannard on the way out. He even smelled comfortable. That's because he smokes the same brand of pipe-tobacco my grandfather smoked. Grandfather was comfortable and safe, she explained to the part of her that had a mad impulse to give Stannard a warm hug. 'And you say he died here?' she asked.

'Yes,' Stannard answered slowly; he was watching her face. 'In bed. He just went to sleep and never woke up. A good way to go in my book.'

Elizabeth raised her eyebrows. She supposed that might be true. Though the thought of sleeping in the house where Uncle Abner had recently died wasn't any too appealing. In her book people died in the hospital . . . if possible.

She followed Stannard up to the second floor. His muscular legs went easily up the steep, narrow stairs. He doesn't have turkey legs, she thought, then dismissed the thought. She certainly wasn't interested in Gare Stannard's legs, she reminded herself. Ted had had skinny legs.

Turkey legs. That's disloyal, Elizabeth, that's definitely disloyal. Stop it. Stop it right this instant!

It was easy to tell that Stannard liked Uncle Abner's house. He spoke of it as though he owned it, and was reluctantly having to part with something very dear to his heart.

It was strange, Elizabeth reflected, being shown around your own property by someone who knew it intimately . . . especially when you had never set foot on it, and weren't planning on ever coming back to look at it again.

'Well, there you have it,' Stannard said when they had completed the tour. He said it expectantly, as though he was waiting for her to say — 'I'll take it!' She didn't know what to say, so she simply thanked him for his time.

Stannard was standing with one hand on the screen door, ready to leave. If he was disappointed in her reply, she couldn't tell. The sun was back-lighting his form, casting a golden-red aura around his head. If she hadn't known better, Elizabeth would have thought him somehow magical. As it was, the house, the day and all that had happened, were catching her up in a spell of some sort. She laughed a nervous little laugh. 'Well, thank you again for all your help, and for showing me MY home . . . I mean house, MY HOUSE,' she corrected herself. 'I guess I can truthfully say, I was fortunate to have almost run into you.'

He laughed, an easy comfortable sound,

well-worn like old shoes of good leather. 'I'll stop by in the morning.' He opened the screen and let it shut gently behind him. 'Goodnight . . . Elizabeth.'

'Goodnight and thanks again.' She almost didn't want him to leave.

Elizabeth stood in the doorway and watched the blue pick-up turn around and head back down the drive. Stannard stuck his arm out of the truck window and waved. She was surprised that he had noticed she was still in the doorway.

Three

Stannard had no more than disappeared down the road when Elizabeth remembered she hadn't called her parents and the children. She had hoped to make her Vermont trip up and back in one long day's time. But since that wasn't going to be possible, she needed to call so nobody would worry. Besides that, she had made a point to tell the children she would call to tell them goodnight and sweet dreams. She looked at her watch. It was almost seven. She'd have to hurry. Stannard's house and the phone were at least a mile down the road.

Momentarily, she considered letting herself forget the whole thing. After all, how important was a simple goodnight call? It wasn't the end of the world. But she knew her parents would worry, and the children would cry. She wasn't the type of person who forgot to do what she said she'd do. And she wasn't the type of person who let other people worry just because she had to walk a mile to a phone. And, she thought ruefully, she also wasn't the type of person who got stuck in some God-forsaken wilderness without a phone either.

Elizabeth rummaged in her flight-bag for her sweater. She was glad she had thought to bring a little something extra. With the sun going down, the air was cooling off. She even thought to turn on a light. The idea of coming back to a totally dark strange house wasn't too inviting.

She flipped the switch near the door. Nothing. 'Maybe this switch is broken,' she said aloud. She tried another. Still no light. 'Well, bright one,' she chided herself, 'of course there's no light. The electricity is turned off!'

She made a mental note to ask Stannard about borrowing a flashlight or at least a candle or two. Then she shut the door and headed jauntily down the driveway.

The sun was behind the mountains, but the sky was still light in the west. She could hear night-birds calling, a sad and lonesome sound in the distance. On the road beneath the trees the shadows were turning to black velvet. It was a soft night coming on, and Elizabeth, who was used to city lights and canyons of concrete, wasn't altogether sure she wasn't afraid of this different sort of night. Irrationally, she thought to herself, what they need out here are a few streetlights. She shivered and pulled her sweater closer around her slim body. 'I will not be afraid,' she spoke out loud. Her voice sounded small and insubstantial, as though the living night was soaking it up. 'There's absolutely nothing to be afraid of out here,' she said with a lot more bravado than she felt. She walked a little faster.

Shortly, she heard the motor of a car approaching. She stepped back off the road into the deeper shadows and stood still. The car

29

whizzed on by her, then skidded to a stop and backed up. Elizabeth froze. A rough-looking young man poked his head out of the car window. 'Breakdown?' he asked.

'No . . . no,' Elizabeth replied.

'Just out for a walk?' he asked pleasantly.

Elizabeth relaxed a little. 'Well, yes,' she answered.

'Fine night for a walk,' he remarked.

Elizabeth nodded. The young man narrowed his eyes, trying to get a better look at her in the fast-fading light. 'You're new around here, aren't you?' he asked.

Elizabeth was alarmed Why was he asking that?

'Don't believe I've ever seen you before,' he continued.

'I'm a friend of Gare Stannard's,' she answered, hoping that the image of big, burly Gare would impress this rather frightening-looking person, whoever he was.

'Stannard . . . the game warden.' The young man half laughed. 'I know him well. He's given me hell a time or two for fishing without a licence.' Elizabeth noted the absence of anger in his voice. 'Tell him Sandy says hello. Now, you watch out for snipes! S'long!' He put the car in gear and took off down the road before Elizabeth could ask about snipes.

What in heaven's name were snipes? Elizabeth peered into the dark woods. She shivered. Whatever they were, they'd have to be pretty fast because she was ready to run. She set off at a fast jog, her eyes now and again scanning the dark canopy of leaves above her head. Maybe it was some sort of bird . . . like bats. She knew bats were supposed to get tangled in your hair.

She hadn't gone far when she heard a strange sound. Just some night-bird, she told herself. I'll ignore it. 'Burrrrr . . . chit!' There it was again! Actually, it didn't sound too frightening, more like a cat with a rubber-band motor. She could hear the crackle of twigs as whatever it was made its way through the underbrush. Elizabeth picked up her pace.

She ran by the spot where her car had been. Evidently the mechanic had come and taken it away. Now she wished he had been a little slower. She would have liked to jump inside and lock the doors. She wasn't used to running and she had a fair distance to go yet.

'Burrrrr . . . urr . . . chit . . . chit,' called the snipe or whatever it was. Elizabeth glanced back. The snipe had come out onto the road. She could dimly see the outline of a small animal body headed her way. It wasn't very big, cat-sized at best. But it definitely wasn't a cat, that much she knew. But if it was a wild animal, why was it coming towards her? Weren't wild animals supposed to run from humans? And hadn't she been told, or read, that wild animals that acted unafraid were very likely to have rabies! Elizabeth broke out in a cold sweat.

Luckily, the snipe couldn't run too fast, or

Elizabeth wouldn't have had the breath to keep going. She came to Stannard's long uphill driveway, and looked back. Maybe the snipe had given up by this time. 'Damn!' No such luck. The little animal was still coming on strong.

Elizabeth took a ragged breath and started up the long drive. Her thin-soled flats weren't meant for running over gravel roads. She especially felt the rocks in Stannard's drive. Her foot rolled sideways over a particularly large stone and she went down hard on one knee.

The snipe churred and gurgled. It sounded positively happy that she was getting down to its level. Elizabeth didn't pause to check the damage done by her fall, or even to check over her shoulder on the progress of the snipe. All she knew was it sounded too close for comfort. Elizabeth got up immediately and struggled on up the hill.

'Stannard! Stannard!' Elizabeth yelled. Nobody appeared. 'Stannard!' she yelled again as she ran up the steps to the porch.

Still no sign that there was anyone in the house.

Elizabeth looked back. The snipe was lumbering up the steps. She pounded on the door. 'Come on, Stannard! Open up!' She looked again. The snipe had made the porch . . . 'Burrrrrrr . . . chit . . . chit!' and was coming for her!

Elizabeth opened the door and stepped inside. 'I'm coming in, Stannard,' she yelled. Then she slammed the screen door and latched it. The snipe stood on the other side of the screen and burred unhappily.

'Go away!' hissed Elizabeth. She had to admit the snipe didn't look particularly ferocious. Up close, it looked rather fuzzy and cute.

Now that she was inside, she could hear water running and a fine tenor voice singing 'Danny Boy'. She knocked loudly on the bathroom door. 'Stannard!'

'Danny Boy' came to an abrupt halt. 'Who's there?'

'It's me, Stannard, Elizabeth Elkins!' she shouted.

'Elizabeth Elkins! What on earth are you doing here?'

'I came to use your phone . . . I got chased by a snipe . . . it's right outside on your porch and . . .'

'A what? Who?' he shouted back.

'Can't you come out here? I can't keep shouting at you.'

The water shut off and she could hear him muttering to himself. Then the bathroom door flew open and there he was dressed in nothing but a towel.

Elizabeth gulped. The look of him caught in her throat. He was a wet six foot plus of supple manly body with a nice sprinkling of hair on his chest. Elizabeth couldn't help but stare. 'You could have at least put on some clothes,' she finally managed to say.

'What and spoil your surprise?' He was grinning at her. He leaned against the door jamb, arms crossed across his chest. Elizabeth was afraid the towel he had tucked around his waist would let go.

'And to what do I owe all this commotion? Or do you always go around bursting into people's houses, interrupting their showers?'

'Burrrrr . . . chit . . . chit,' said the snipe at the door.

'That's part of it,' Elizabeth answered quickly. 'That . . . that snipe creature chased me here!'

'Snipe creature?' Stannard walked over to the door and turned on the porch light. Elizabeth's eyes followed the working of the muscles in his wide shoulders and back. Heated thoughts flitted through her mind. How was that towel staying put? What if it fell off? Where should she put her eyes?

'Hello, little fellow,' Stannard said to the snipe. His voice was soft and mellow. Clearly, he didn't think the snipe was cause for alarm.

He turned around and the loosely wrapped towel slipped. He neatly caught it before it fell too low. But he didn't miss the look of what was it — guilty anticipation — in Elizabeth's eyes. 'Who told you this was a snipe?' he asked.

'A bearded fellow on the road.' Elizabeth was aware of the flush on her cheeks. Why was this Stannard person rattling her usual calm and re- serve? He was just a man, an ordinary, nice-looking man. Nothing to get so addle-pated about. 'He said his name was Sandy. He said he knew you, that you had given him the devil for fishing without a licence.'

'Sandy Audet,' smiled Stannard. 'And he told you this was a snipe?'

'Not exactly.' Elizabeth looked away again, and noticed for the first time that she had torn her brand-new slacks. Damn. Why didn't he get dressed? 'He said to look out for snipes.'

'And?' Stannard prompted.

'And then this creature appeared and started chasing me down the road.'

'You were out on the road . . . again?'

'Yes,' Elizabeth answered somewhat hotly. 'I was walking down the road. Where else do you think I would have been?'

'So, you were taking an evening stroll down the road, and ran into Sandy Audet, who said look out for snipes?'

Elizabeth gritted her teeth. Why was this Stannard person so difficult to get along with? All she wanted was to make a simple phone call and he was making some sort of federal case out of it. She resisted the urge to yell at him. As calmly as she could, she explained: 'After you left, I remembered I had to call my parents and my children. I was simply coming here to use your phone!' In spite of her good intentions, she had raised her voice.

'Now, now, Liza,' he said soothingly. 'No need to get all bent out of shape over this . . . eh, snipe incident.' He was quiet for a moment or two. 'You never went to camp, when you were a kid, did you?'

'What are you talking about?' she almost shouted at him.

'Calm down, Liza. I only asked a simple question.' He was still grinning at her.

'I can't see what my going to camp has to do with anything! And my name is Elizabeth, not Liza, thank you!'

'My, my, you are excitable.' Nothing seemed to put a dent in his easy-going good-humour. 'First of all let me say, you are welcome to use my phone. But it seems to me this is no way to treat a knight in shining armour, who rescues you from broken cars, phonelessness and snipes.' His grin had broken out into a wide smile. He was certainly enjoying himself at her expense.

'Knights in shining armour,' she spit out the words, 'don't parade around in bath-towels!'

'Have you forgotten, my dear Liza, that you were the one who came here, let yourself in, and pounded on my bathroom door? I wasn't exactly expecting the pleasure of your company.'

'Stop calling me Liza,' she answered lamely. He was right of course. Damn him. Everything he said was true. She had done all of that and more.

'Elizabeth simply doesn't fit,' he went on in his maddeningly calm way. 'My grandmother's name was Elizabeth and she was a refined and gentle lady. Never in her wildest dreams would she have roared into someone's life the way you've roared into mine . . . and all in one day too.' He winked at her. 'I just can't think of you as Elizabeth. Whatever you are, you're definitely not an Elizabeth.' He smiled like the proverbial Cheshire cat.

Elizabeth simply shook her head in helplessness. He was impossible. This whole situation was impossible. Suddenly, she felt very tired. Her knee throbbed. She just wanted to make her call and go home to bed. Home? Back to Abner's house. Heaven only knew what sort of bats and snakes and snipes were awaiting her there. But at least there she'd have peace and quiet, and not be roaring into anyone's life, as Stannard put it. 'May I use your phone?' she asked in a weary voice.

'Of course,' he answered. 'You know where it is. And I'll go get some clothes on. Maybe things will go more smoothly . . .' he let his voice trail off. She glanced over at him. He had been waiting for her to look his way. He gave her a big wink.

Before she thought about it, she stuck out her tongue.

He headed for the bathroom laughing merrily. 'Liza, definitely a Liza!'

Josh answered the phone. 'We've been waiting for your call, Mommy.' Elizabeth said a silent prayer that she had decided to call. 'What's it like in Vermont?' he went on. 'Gramma says they've got mountains and trout streams and loads of wild animals. Did you see any wild animals?'

'A few,' she answered, trying to sound as low-key as possible.

'Like what?'

'Oh, skunks and snipes,' she answered.

'Raccoons,' Stannard called from the bathroom door. He was just zipping up his pants. Elizabeth quickly lowered her eyes.

'What's a snipe?' asked Josh.

'A little furry, fuzzy animal,' Elizabeth answered.

'It's a raccoon,' Stannard said again.

'A raccoon?' repeated Elizabeth.

'A raccoon? A snipe is a raccoon?' questioned Josh.

'I was talking to someone else,' Elizabeth told her son.

'You were talking to a raccoon?' Josh asked in amazement.

'No,' Elizabeth answered patiently. 'I wasn't talking to a raccoon.'

'You might as well have been,' Stannard chuckled.

'Be quiet!' snapped Elizabeth.

'But, Mommy . . .'

'I wasn't talking to you, Josh. I was talking to someone here . . . where I'm using the phone.'

'Who?' asked Josh, who always liked to get to the bottom of things.

'A man named Gare Stannard,' Elizabeth answered.

'Who's he?'

'He's the person who owns the phone I'm using.'

'And he has raccoons?' Josh's voice was edged with excitement.

'No . . . well, I don't know if he has raccoons,' Elizabeth replied.

'Sometimes I have raccoons,' Stannard said loudly enough for the boy to hear.

'Mom, he has raccoons! I heard him say that!'

'Well, he's a game warden,' she answered matter-of-factly. 'I suppose game wardens sometimes have raccoons.' She hoped that would be the end of that.

'Oh Mom, a real game warden. Can I talk to him?'

'No,' said Elizabeth, 'he's very busy.'

'Please, Mommy,' begged Josh. 'Just for a minute.'

Elizabeth looked up at Stannard. He was standing with his hands in his pockets, his head tipped slightly to one side. She could tell he was probably making a fairly accurate guess at what Josh was asking.

'Please, Mommy,' Josh pleaded again.

'Just a minute, Josh,' Elizabeth sighed. She put her hand over the receiver and spoke to Stannard. 'My son seems to be enthralled by your occupation. He'd like to speak to a real game warden.'

Stannard took the receiver. 'I'd be honoured,' he said, and it was easy to hear in his tone of voice that he meant it.

Gare and Josh seemed to hit it off immediately. Elizabeth let her mind and eyes wander. Stannard's home was so well decorated. Somebody with a good eye for colour and design had had a hand in decorating it. She wondered if it could possibly have been done by the man of the house himself.

'Hello, Trudy,' said Stannard. He smiled at Elizabeth's questioning eyes, then went on to talk to Trudy. Elizabeth answered him with a rueful smile and a shake of her head. Here, *she* had called her children and who was doing all the talking?

She was beginning to think maybe Stannard was right. Maybe she wasn't Elizabeth after all. Maybe she was Alice. Maybe she had fallen down a rabbit-hole into a strange topsy-turvy Wonderland of Vermont, where things were completely upside-down, and not the way they should be at all, and nothing was what it seemed. Maybe this was all a bad dream and in a moment or two she'd wake up in her own bed in her apartment in New York and things would be back to normal.

'Here,' said Stannard, thrusting the phone towards her. 'It's your mother.'

Elizabeth took the phone. 'Hello, Mother?'

'Hello, dear,' her mother's familiar voice came over the wire. 'Such a pleasant young man! I'm so glad you've managed to meet someone who can give you a hand. He says he knew Abner well. Isn't that a great piece of luck?'

'Yes, Mother,' Elizabeth answered in a strained voice. She could easily read between her mother's lines. Her mother was always and forever matchmaking. 'It's not good for you to be alone, Elizabeth. And the children need a father. Think of the children.' How many times had she heard those lines in the last three years since Ted had been killed in an auto accident? Sight unseen, her mother had probably already filled Stannard into the spot of groom in that ongoing wedding she was planning and plotting in her head.

Her mother had managed to introduce her to every eligible, or even marginally eligible, male she could lay hands on. It wouldn't have surprised Elizabeth to learn that her mother ran ads in newspapers. Elizabeth fully expected to see her plight advertised in a double-page spread some Sunday morning in *The New York Times*.

Just for instance, there had been a very elaborate dinner-party set up so that Elizabeth could meet a wispy, uncertain young man, the son of one of her mother's old friends. Even her mother, when pressed, couldn't find much to recommend about his prospects. 'He's . . . he's . . .' Elizabeth thought that her mother was at long last stymied on this particular specimen. 'He's got a fine mother!' she said at last. Elizabeth howled with laughter.

Elizabeth had often thought that if there was such a thing as reincarnation, then her mother had most certainly been a matchmaker in every one of her previous lives.

Her father was a little better. At least he didn't actively go out beating the bushes for eligible husband/ father material. All he'd do was smile indulgently when she complained. 'Listen to your mother, Elizabeth. She's a wise woman.'

Elizabeth loved her parents dearly, it was just they were impossible when it came to the subject of Elizabeth Must Have Another Husband . . . the sooner the better!

Elizabeth quickly changed the subject. She told her mother about the car. And though the old station-wagon was like another child in the family to her mother, she seemed hardly worried about the damage it had sustained to its tyre and radiator. It had brought a reasonably nice-sounding man, who obviously must like children, into Elizabeth's life. That was what mattered. That was what counted.

Elizabeth said goodnight to Trudy and to Josh. Much to her consternation, both children kept repeating back to her what Stannard had told them.

When she finally was able to hang up, she turned around to find Stannard at the door. He had let the little creature in. The fuzzy little thing was stuffing crackers in its mouth as fast as it could chew them. 'Do all snipes behave like this one?'

'Raccoons, this is a young raccoon. And to answer your question, no. This little fellow, as you can see, is very used to humans. He was undoubtedly raised by some well-meaning people. And then when he got to this size, which corresponds roughly to the 'terrible-twos' in a human child, they dumped him in the woods. It happens more often than I like to think about.'

'Why dump him, as you put it?'

'Because while coons are exceptionally intriguing pets, they're also crafty, intelligent, and one hundred and ten per cent determination. By the time they're several months old, they're a real handful. It can come down to — either the coon goes or we go — in a big hurry.

Elizabeth watched the coon carefully pick up a shred of cracker in its hand-like paws. 'He eats as though he's starved.'

'He was. He's too young to fend for himself. Poor little fellow. Imagine being dumped in the woods at the tender age of two. You'd have no idea what to eat.'

'And then I came along,' Elizabeth continued for him. 'And he thought — Oh boy . . . people . . . FOOD!'

'Right,' chuckled Stannard. 'And because Sandy had told you to watch out for snipes, you thought a hungry little animal charging after you was nothing to fool with.'

'Yes,' said Elizabeth. She had thought he might make fun of her and she was glad that he hadn't. 'Just what is a snipe?'

'A bird.'

'A bird? Only a bird?'

'A shy meadow and swamp bird. Nothing at

43

all to be afraid of. Sandy's snipe, on the other hand, is a mythological creature that hangs around children's camps and the like. It's meant to scare and trick.' Stannard was grinning.

'Explain please,' Elizabeth asked crisply.

'One of the best traditional tricks played on beginning campers is to take them on a snipe hunt. You give each one an empty pillow-case and a flashlight, and take them out into the dark woods beyond the security of the campfire light. Then you find them a good spot on a 'snipe' run and you tell them to hold open the pillow-case until a snipe runs in. They aren't to come back to camp until they've caught a snipe. It's sort of a rite of passage for campers.'

'And there's no such thing as a snipe?'

'Right.'

'Sounds sorta mean.'

'Not really. Not when it's been done to everyone. There's a camaraderie about having passed the test, and being a good sport about it.'

'Well, maybe,' Elizabeth allowed.

'If it's any consolation,' Stannard was grinning at her, 'I think we can say you passed yours.'

'Thanks,' she answered drily.

'You're welcome.' He picked up the little coon, which by now seemed almost full of crackers. 'You've got nice kids.' He looked at her almost shyly from under his great dark brows.

'Thank you.'

'You and your husband are lucky.'

'My husband was killed in an accident three years ago.'

'I'm sorry,' he said simply.

'Me too,' she answered.

He looked at her a moment as though he was trying to decide what manner of bird or beast she might be. 'Let's put this little fellow to bed and then I'll give you a lift back to Abner's.'

She followed him out to a small barn behind the house. He put the little coon in a strong cage, filled the water-dish, and put in an old shirt to make a comfortable bed.

'Why a cage?'

'Because of the trouble he could get into on his own. And for his safety.'

Elizabeth was almost beginning to wish she was a little raccoon that someone named Gare Stanndard was taking care of. A cage in the barn with an old shirt for a bed might even be preferable to Abner's dark and ghostly house right now.

A bright full moon had risen by the time they reached Abner's house. Gare rummaged around in the glove compartment for a flashlight. Elizabeth halfway hoped he didn't have one. Maybe he'd invite her back to his house. She could really do with a clean, well-lighted room right now . . . one with the sound of another human voice. She was too tired to be brave.

'Here it is.' Gare pulled out the flashlight. He switched it on. The beam was steady and strong.

'Come on,' Gare said cheerfully. 'Let's get you settled.'

Gare found an oil-lamp in the pantry. He expertly trimmed the wick and lighted it. A warm, golden glow filled the old kitchen. 'There you are,' he beamed in the lamplight. His face was somehow comforting. Two tiny lamps were reflected in his soft brown eyes. Elizabeth kept watch over the tiny lamps for a second too long. Gare leaned an inch or two nearer and she quickly drew her eyes aside. He reached over and touched the back of her head, kissing her ever so lightly on the top of her head. 'Take care,' he said softly. 'I'll see you in the morning.' He stepped to the door and turned. 'You're quite safe here, you know.'

His face looked so dear in the lamplight. Elizabeth wanted to call him back. She could still feel the touch of his fingers and his lips in her hair. There was electricity in him. He had ignited something in her. He had called forth something strange and wonderful. No, she told herself severely. You're overtired. Tomorrow things will look different. Tomorrow you will be sorry if you step out of line tonight. She put steely politeness in her voice — 'Goodnight, and thank you again.'

Elizabeth was too exhausted to be any more adventuresome. She simply blew out the lamp and laid down on the day-bed in the kitchen. Any port in a storm, she told herself, wondering just how much sleep she'd get in a strange house, in a strange bed, in a strange land.

Four

She couldn't believe it when she awoke to the smell of fresh coffee brewing. Bright sun was streaming in the windows. She looked at her watch — half past nine! She never slept that late. Was she imagining that coffee? No, there was a carafe of coffee over on the stove. Stannard! Either Stannard had been there, or Uncle Abner's ghost had fixed coffee.

She walked stiffly over to the sink. Her knee was sore. She rolled up her pant leg to look at the damage in the light of day. The skin was only slightly nicked in a few little spots. Nothing to worry about. She rolled the pant leg back down and reached to turn on a tap. No water. Evidently, that was turned off too. There was an old-fashioned pump mounted beside the sink. She worked the handle up and down. Things gurgled and gulped and out came a stream of water. She said a silent thank you to Abner for his old-fashioned ways, and washed her face and hands in the bracing cold water.

She found a fresh towel in a drawer beside the sink, just where she imagined towels ought to be. She smiled. It was a strange link between herself and a dead man. But she felt right then that she was beginning to know Uncle Abner.

She heard whistling outside. She stepped to the window. It was little panes of wobbly glass that turned the view slightly askew, almost like a kaleidoscope. Elizabeth had had a kaleidoscope as a kid. You put it up to your eye and it turned the world on its ear, turned the rational, orderly world into bits and pieces of crazy quilt colour. This kaleidoscope window turned Gare Stannard into a disjointed figure. She went to the door to meet him, a smile on her face.

'Ah-ha, good-morning, sleepy-head!' he greeted her warmly. His hands were full of flowers. 'I brought some wild flowers for Sleeping Beauty. I thought you might be working on your first hundred years.'

'What?'

'Sleeping Beauty slept for one hundred years, didn't she?' He was grinning down at her. The nearness of him made her world seem suddenly larger, better somehow.

She remembered that she hadn't brushed her hair. And she felt self-conscious about how rumpled her clothes must look. 'I feel a century older too,' she answered.

'No matter,' he replied crisply. "That's easily remedied. I see you didn't eat anything last night. What you need is breakfast, Stannard style. Here,' he thrust the flowers at her, 'find something to put these in. Look in the pantry on the top shelf. I think Abner kept some jugs up there. And while you do that, I'll fix breakfast.'

'But . . . but . . . everything is turned off. There's no water in the taps and no electricity.'

'But there's water in the hand-dug well and

there's gas in the tank for the stove. Abner was a crafty old cuss. He wasn't about to let the electric company or anyone else dictate his life.'

'Smart,' said Elizabeth. She very much admired independent people.

'Yes, I think so,' Stannard agreed with hearty conviction.

Stannard began bustling about the kitchen, while Elizabeth went to find a container for the flowers. She came back with a large earthenware pitcher with an indistinct blue flower on its side.

She probably wouldn't have paid too much attention to the pitcher, if she hadn't singled it out for the flowers. She set the flowers in the middle of the kitchen table. The sun flooded in and danced among the blossoms. She stepped back to admire the bouquet. The whole setting looked like something in one of those early American home-decorating magazines.

Stannard was busily frying bacon in a large black iron skillet. He turned to look too. 'Perfect! They look just right in that pancake pitcher.'

'Pancake pitcher?'

'That's an antique pancake-batter pitcher.'

Elizabeth had never paid much attention to antiques. She and Ted had decided on modern furniture. They had both admired the sleek, cool, uncluttered lines of modern design. 'Wouldn't that hold an awful lot of batter?' she asked.

'Of course,' Stannard answered. 'Farm wives

had a lot of mouths to feed. The families were often large and then there were the hired men to feed too.'

Elizabeth shuddered. 'Those wives, they died young, I suppose?'

'Some did. Some of the men did too . . . and the children. Medicine wasn't very advanced in those days. But my great-grandmother Stannard lived to be ninety-two. She was a farm wife, one of the old-fashioned kind. She and great-grandfather had nine children.'

'The poor thing.' Elizabeth could just imagine the drudgery and hardships great-grandmother Stannard had endured.

'You wouldn't have said that if you had known her,' Stannard answered carefully. He turned to regard Elizabeth with a critical eye. 'She was one of the happiest, sunniest people I've ever known. She loved life. She always said — "I've had a good life. The Lord has truly blessed me." '

Elizabeth raised her eyebrows. 'Maybe she didn't have anything else to compare it to. After all, women didn't have the opportunities then that they have now.'

'If you're suggesting she didn't know any better, you're wrong. Her father was a banker, very well-to-do. She could have sat on her fanny and been a pampered lady of leisure if she had cared to. Actually, she could have been anything she wanted. She had the drive and grit. And she had parents that saw to it that she had a good ed-ucation. They were what you'd call enlightened.

Great-grandmother was brought up to make her own decisions. She chose to become a farm wife. I don't think she was ever sorry, not from what I ever heard or saw of her.'

'Well,' said Elizabeth, 'maybe she was just lucky.'

'Maybe,' Stannard answered lightly. He flipped the eggs over expertly. Elizabeth wasn't about to tell him that that was a feat beyond her. She always broke the yolks.

They sat down to a delicious breakfast. Whatever else Stannard might be, he was also a very good short-order cook. Elizabeth dug in with relish. Everything tasted so good. She hadn't realized how hungry she was.

'Should I make more?'

Elizabeth looked up from her nearly empty plate and blushed. She had been doing what she always told the children not to do — she had gobbled her food. 'Oh no . . . I'm sorry . . . my manners are dreadful . . .'

'Don't bother to apologize,' Stannard waved her protests aside. 'You and the little coon have something in common, both hungry babes lost in the wood.'

She wondered if she should protest his use of the word 'babes'. In her city-forged feminism, the word rankled. But she looked at the open frankness of his face, and decided against it. She smiled at him instead.

'You've got a nice smile, Liza Elkins.'

She coloured slightly. She could feel the

creeping warmth in her neck. 'My name really isn't Liza,' she answered calmly.

'I know, you told me,' he answered equally as calmly. 'But I just cannot call you Elizabeth. Do you want me to call you Mrs Elkins?'

'Well, no,' she replied. She didn't quite dare look directly into those soft brown eyes.

'What's your middle name? Maybe that's a possibility,' he suggested in his somehow soothing voice.

'It's awful.' She glanced up at him.

'Oh? Mine too,' he chuckled. 'I'll make you a deal. You tell me yours and I'll tell you mine.'

Elizabeth had to smile. They sounded like two little kids playing doctor. You show me YOURS and I'll show you MINE. Why did her mind slip into body parts when they were talking names? 'It's Cassandra,' she answered with a grimace. 'My mother had an aunt Cassandra.'

'Cassandra,' he repeated. "That's not so bad. Sure beats Waldo.'

'Waldo?'

'Yep. I can't tell you the lengths I went to to keep that name a secret. I think I spent my entire childhood in fear that it would somehow leak out.'

She laughed. She couldn't imagine anyone calling Gare Stannard — Waldo. 'Why Waldo?'

'My mother loved Ralph Waldo Emerson. She could have at least picked the Emerson and not the Waldo. I always swore I'd change it when I grew up.'

'Why didn't you?'

'Oh, I don't know. Because my mother chose it, I suppose. She died when I was sixteen. I guess it's just a way to honour her memory. It's a funny thing about names. Take this handsome flower,' he touched a long-stalked plant with single blue flowers up the stem. Feathery bright red stamens projected from each blue centre. 'This is a viper's bugloss. Not a very pretty name for a very pretty flower. Whenever I complained about my name, my mother would always say — "Handsome is as handsome does." '

'Do you know the name of this one?' Elizabeth pointed to another blue flower. This one had white stamens in the centre.

'That's Jacob's-ladder,' he answered.

'And this?'

'Wild sweet-william.'

'Do you know them all?'

'Let's see. Dame's-rocket, loosestrife, trefoil, Turk's cap, buttercup, tansy and Queen Anne's lace,' he named the rest.

'I'm impressed,' she shook her head. 'How do you remember all of that?'

He leaned back in his chair and regarded her with those grand brown eyes. 'Because I want to,' he answered simply.

Elizabeth looked at all six feet plus of him. She had never met a man before who cared to remember the names of wildflowers. Ted wouldn't have cared to remember the names of wildflowers. Ted wouldn't have cared, nor would he have cooked breakfast for her. Not even if she was sick. And he always called her Elizabeth.

'How about Cassie?' asked Stannard. 'I could call you Cassie. That fits, I think.'

'Cassie?' She turned the strange name over in her head. 'I'll have to think about it,' she answered. She supposed it didn't really matter what he wanted to call her. She wasn't going to be around here much longer anyway. He was pleasant. This was pleasant. But she had things to do with her life. Her life was in the city . . . going to school . . . taking care of the kids . . . seeing that they all stayed 'on track' — that was a favourite expression of Ted's. She and Ted had mapped out their lives, and the children's too. It was a good plan. And just because Ted wasn't around to see it through, was no reason to drop the plan. People needed framework to their lives. That's how you completed your goals. That's how you made something of yourself. Ted was the organizer. She had been the one who was all loose ends until Ted came along and changed all that. Ted had made her see that she was simply frittering her life away with no goals.

'Now, about my car,' she said, getting up and stacking the dishes.

'Oh, I meant to tell you. Tommy called this morning and said he wouldn't have the parts until Monday morning.'

'Monday morning!' she almost shouted.

'Don't yell at me,' he shrugged. 'It's not my fault.'

'I know, I know.' She tried to calm her irritation. 'But Monday! What am I supposed to do until Monday?'

'Search me.' He was almost grinning. 'Here, let me help you with those.' He took the plates out of her hands. 'Maybe you can entertain your mom and dad and the kids.'

'What?'

'That was another call,' he said on his way to the sink. 'Your mom and dad and the children are driving up today.'

'Oh no! You're kidding! They aren't!' she groaned.

'No, I'm not kidding. And yes, they are,' he answered. She couldn't see his face, but she could hear the smile in his voice. It made her mad.

'And you didn't tell them not to come?' she demanded.

'You expect me to tell your mother and father what to do?'

'You . . . you . . . you're impossible!' she exploded. 'They can't come here! This is no place for them. No running water. No electricity. Come on, we're going to your house to call them back right now!'

'You can call if it'll make you feel any better,' he continued in a maddeningly even tone, 'but it won't do any good. They've left already.'

'How do you know?' she asked through gritted teeth. How could he be so offhanded about things?

'Look . . . Cassie,' he tried out the new name,

55

which of course made her all the more angry. 'They called very early. Before seven. They were all set to walk out the door then. There wasn't much I could do about it except tell you, which I've done.' He tried not to grin at her, but he couldn't quite help it. He quite obviously thought she was all tempest in a teapot.

'Stop grinning at me! It's not funny!'

'Okay,' he said easily. He turned around and began to pump water into the sink to do the dishes.

'Leave them alone,' she directed sternly. 'I'll do them. They're my dishes and I'll do them.'

'Fine. Suit yourself,' he answered. He dried his hands and looked at her. She looked away. He was no longer smiling.

'Don't you have to go to work or something?' she asked, her voice still too full of anger and frustration.

'It's Saturday. But yes, I have things to do.' He walked to the door. 'Nice to have met you . . . Mrs Elkins.' He didn't slam the door. She would have. But his voice was tight. Then he got in his blue pick-up and drove down the drive. He didn't turn in the direction of his house, but the other way.

Elizabeth stood back away from the door so he couldn't see her watching. Almost as soon as he had vanished from sight, her anger vanished too. In its place was guilt. She had behaved badly. Very badly. She wondered if she'd ever see him again. And she wondered why it suddenly seemed to matter a great deal to her that she did.

Five

Tears welled up in Elizabeth's eyes. How had her life gotten so completely out of hand? All she had set out to do was look at Uncle Abner's house. She knew it made good business sense to know the worth of the property before she sold it. She sniffed and blew her nose. It was almost as if something or someone had got hold of her life and was forcing her to do things she didn't want to do.

'Listen here, Uncle Abner,' she said out loud, 'if this is your doing, I'll have you know I am an independent woman and I will do as I jolly well want with this place and with my life!' So saying, she stamped her foot and set off upstairs to find some sheets and blankets for the beds.

She was surprised to find the bedding all neatly stacked and folded just where she thought it should be. 'Okay, Uncle Abner,' she continued to talk out loud, 'so you know where sheets should be kept . . . so what!' She shook her finger at the ceiling where she thought any self-respecting ghost might be lurking. 'You won't trick me into liking you and this place just because you put sheets away where I would.' She wasn't talking to Uncle Abner because she believed in ghosts, she told herself, but because it made her feel better to hear words echoing in the house . . . even if they were her own words.

She marched into a front bedroom and began

making up the bed. She fluffed the pillows and opened the window. Her eyes searched the road in both directions for a blue pick-up. 'I don't care if Stannard never comes back,' she said to a pillow. 'It's just too bad to have things end on a sour note, that's all.' She socked the pillow square in the middle and smoothed the spread.

At the door she paused and looked back into the room. The curtains gently blowing at the open window, the oak dresser with acorn handles, the antique bed with fresh white sheets, everything looked old-fashioned and inviting. 'So, you look lovely,' she said to the empty room, 'that just means you'll sell well!'

The breeze, as though in answer, blew a gust that whined through the shutters.

'Save your breath, Uncle Abner. You won't change my mind!' She slammed the door.

When she had made beds enough, she pounded down the stairs. Her fierce determination made the stairs creak in annoyance.

She was further annoyed when she found the broom in the first place she looked. She swept the kitchen and glared at Gare's lovely wildflowers. 'You won't change my mind either, you tansy and Queen . . . whoever's . . . lace.' She couldn't remember the flower names and that annoyed her too.

It wasn't long before she heard the sound of car doors slamming and Trudy's excited little voice calling — 'Mommy, Mommy, Mommy where are you?' Elizabeth went to the door and watched her daughter skip up the fieldstone path to Uncle Abner's house. Josh, being typically Josh, was behind Trudy, walking first backward and then forward, so as not to miss seeing anything. And bringing up the rear were her mother and father, laden with an ice-chest and bundles.

'Hello, dear, this place is beautiful,' gushed her mother.

'A gem!' agreed her father.

'It's just right!' said Trudy, sounding like a line from her favourite *The Three Bears*.

'Can we keep it?' Josh asked, his eyes serious.

'Well, the electricity is turned off and there's only the hand-dug well for water. I hope you all are ready to rough it.'

'Lead me to it,' her father laughed good-naturedly.

'Stannard should have told you what you were in for,' Elizabeth went on. 'It's quite primitive. No water means no bathroom. You'll have to use the three-holer.' She indicated the outhouse at the edge of the back lawn.

If she had expected her mother's face to sour at the thought of an outdoor privy, she was mistaken. Her mother kept right on smiling. 'The best vacation we ever had was before you were born, Elizabeth dear. We had a log cabin up in the Michigan woods — a three-holer — a campfire for cooking — a birch-bark canoe and a crystal-clear lake. It was heaven!'

Elizabeth raised her eyebrows in reluctant surprise. 'Well, Stannard should have told you all the same.'

'But he did, dear,' said her mother. 'He said we should be forewarned that it was quite primitive, didn't he, dear?'

'I believe he said it was rustic,' answered her husband.

'That's it,' she agreed, 'rustic.' She said the word as though it was something fine and luxurious that she was speaking of.

Elizabeth couldn't believe her ears. She shrugged, then sighed and kissed them all. The children, with her father in tow, ran off to try out Uncle Abner's swing.

Elizabeth murmured apologies while she helped her mother unpack the mountains of food they had brought. 'I'm sorry you felt you had to come and rescue me. I'm a big girl now. I can handle life's little emergencies. I'm sorry if I gave you the wrong impression.'

'No-no-no, dear,' her mother waved away the apologies. 'We didn't come to rescue our little girl, never fear. We came on a lark.'

'A lark?'

'You know, an adventure. A farm in Vermont sounds so romantic. We wanted to see it for ourselves. Now, where is that nice young man we spoke to on the phone?'

'Home, I suppose.' Elizabeth rolled her eyes. 'He has a home. He doesn't live here, Mother. He's simply a friendly neighbour . . . or was . . .' She paused, realizing too late that she had said more than she had intended.

'What do you mean by "or was"?'

'We had a small disagreement,' Elizabeth said lightly.

'You mean, don't you,' said her mother, 'that you've run him off . . . just as you've done to every other eligible man you've met since Ted died. I hate to say this to you, Elizabeth, but you've made a shrine out of your marriage to Ted. Ted was a nice person. And I know you and he had a pretty good marriage . . . but it wasn't perfect. It doesn't deserve to be enshrined for all time as the perfect union no other can touch.'

'Mother, how could you?'

'I can because I love you, my darling daughter.' She reached over and took Elizabeth's hand in hers. 'I see you dedicating your life to the plan you and Ted worked out to the exclusion of everything else and everyone else. I know you think I'm being disrespectful to the dead, and all that, but the fact remains, my dear, dear daughter, that you're alive . . . the children are alive. And it's really all right to live and enjoy life. You don't have to feel guilty about looking for happiness.'

Elizabeth was in tears.

'Now, Elizabeth, I want you to think about what I've said. I'm going outside with your father and your children to try that wonderful swing.' Her mother gently squeezed her hand, then turned and without a backward glance, walked briskly out of the kitchen.

Elizabeth sat down and felt like dissolving on the spot. What was happening? Her life seemed to be falling apart in every direction. She tried to think about it logically but her mind refused to co-operate. She was immensely sad and hurt. And she was angry. How could her mother say those things? How could she?

The screen door banged shut and her father came whistling into the kitchen. 'Need to wet my whistle,' he grinned. 'Swinging is thirsty work.'

Elizabeth pointed to the hand-pump at the sink. 'You'll have to pump yourself a glass.'

The old pump gurgled and gulped and out splashed a stream of water. Her father filled his glass and drank deeply. 'Ahhhhh, good fresh well-water. Water as water was meant to be.' He looked at her solemn face. 'What's wrong, Elizabeth?'

'Mother's mean,' she answered.

'No,' said her father, setting his empty glass on the drainboard. 'Your mother is never mean. I've known her, girl and woman, for over fifty years. She's never been mean. If you think she's mean, you've misunderstood. I guarantee it.'

'Absolutely?' she asked.

'Positively,' he answered. 'Why don't you come on out and try the swing?' he asked gently. 'Might as well, you know, you own it.'

The rest of the day went somewhat better. The children were so delighted with a yard to play in that they tried to stretch every bit of the day just as far as it would go. Elizabeth couldn't help but

62

enjoy their delight. When bedtime could be put off no longer, Elizabeth expected them to be fearful in a house full of candle-lit shadows. To her amazement Trudy said — 'Mommy, this is a friendly house.'

'Yes,' Josh agreed, 'it feels like it likes us. Can we stay here, Mom?'

'Yes, can we? Can we?' Trudy chimed in, clapping her hands.

'I don't know, but I doubt it,' Elizabeth answered.

'Oh Mom,' Josh said in disappointment. 'This is the best place we've ever been in our whole lives.'

'Our whole lives, the bestest,' Trudy parroted with big eyes.

'I'll think about it,' Elizabeth answered. 'Now, you two get some sleep or you'll sleep right through tomorrow and miss it altogether.'

The two children snuggled down immediately and shut their eyes. They were taking no chances. Before Elizabeth was out of the bedroom door, they were asleep.

The fresh air and outdoor play with the children, along with the sleepy candlelight, made the adults happy to go to bed just after nine. There was no more mention of Elizabeth's sombre lifestyle or penchant for running off men, for which Elizabeth was profoundly thankful.

Elizabeth blew out her candle and climbed between the crisp white sheets. The bed felt wonderful. It's just my tiredness, not that Uncle Abner has extra specially fine beds, she told herself. The bed smelled wonderful too. In her tired mind she turned over the problem of how Uncle Abner could have sheets that smelled of wind and flowers. Probably some new anti-static dryer product, she decided. Just before she fell asleep, she knew what it was. Of course, Uncle Abner dried his sheets outdoors. It was fresh air and sunshine she was smelling.

Her tired mind drifted off to sleep and almost immediately began dreaming.

'Cassie, Cassie, get up. Rouse your old bones, my fine lady.'

'No, no.' She pushed whoever it was away.

'You've got to get up, wife o' mine. Who's agoing to feed all our young'uns if you don't?'

Elizabeth peered out from under the blankets. 'How many do we have?' she asked.

It was Stannard standing over her, but he looked much older. His brown hair was quite grey. He was smiling kindly. 'Why Cassie, my sweet, we got so many you plum forgot, haven't you? With Lukey and Suky, the twins, that makes sixteen.' He reached out and touched her breast under her nightgown. His touch was gentle and caressing. It aroused an immediate need in her. 'Ah Cassie, love light of my life, this is what causes all them young'uns to come poppin' into our life. You and me make such beautiful children together.' So saying, he unbuckled his belt and slipped off his pants and climbed in beside her. His strong hard body next to hers made her ache to be possessed.

Just as they were about to consummate their burning desires, there was a rude knock on the door.

'Don't listen,' Elizabeth pleaded. 'Don't hear.'

But the knocking increased in volume. A voice on the other side, that Elizabeth recognized immediately as Ted's, called out — 'I know what you're doing in there. You're being frivolous! You're making love! You're making babies! You can't even afford the ones you've got! You fools! You colossal fools! I've come to foreclose on your farm and you're making love!'

The door flew open. Elizabeth grabbed the bedclothes to cover their nakedness. Ted stood there dressed in black, twirling his pencil-thin moustache like a villain in an old melodrama. 'Ah-ha!' he said, right on cue.

'What are you doing here?' Elizabeth asked. 'You aren't supposed to be here. My mother said you weren't supposed to be here!'

Next to the bed was a nightstand. On the nightstand was the pancake pitcher filled with Stannard's wildflowers. As villain Ted lunged, Elizabeth grabbed the pitcher of wildflowers and brought it crashing down on his head.

When she blinked, she found herself looking down into Ted's coffin. He was covered with flowers, dripping with wildflowers. Elizabeth woke up sobbing.

Moonlight was shining in the window, silvering the old pine floors and making blue shadows on the bed. Elizabeth sat up and looked out across the meadows bathed in moonlight. A breeze was singing sleepy water songs in the maples in the yard. Far in the distance, the Green Mountains had put on their blue night-caps. All was peaceful and serene. A night-bird called its sad refrain. As Elizabeth listened, it seemed to be saying — 'Aaaallaaall right, aaallaaall right.'

For a long while Elizabeth let her tired mind and heart float out on the peaceful night scene. Just before she fell asleep, the thought that she owed Stannard an apology came into her mind. Tomorrow, tomorrow I'll go find him and apologize, she promised herself. That settled, she fell into a dreamless sleep.

Six

When Elizabeth awoke the sun was streaming in the window. She could hear the piping sweet voices of her children rising through the leaves of the maples in the front yard. She looked at her watch — almost nine-thirty! She had slept late again. There was something about the air in Vermont, she decided, that invited sleep. That was another good reason why she could never live in Vermont. She couldn't afford to be so lazy. Nine-thirty. Why, the day was half gone.

As she was dressing, the memory of last night's dream came back to her. Sixteen children and Lukey and Suky, the twins! She chuckled to herself. Imagine her and Stannard with sixteen kids and being ready, able and willing to work on another one! She had to agree with the villainous Ted on that one. That certainly was crazy and shades of fiddling while Rome burned! She wished she could share her dream with someone. It would be good for a laugh, even if in the end it had made her cry. But she didn't feel there was anyone at the moment she could safely tell it to.

Her mother and father were seated at the kitchen table when she came downstairs. They were sipping coffee and speaking softly together but she couldn't quite catch their words.

'Why, good-morning, glory!' her mother greeted her brightly.

'Sleep well?' asked her father.

'Yes. How about you, Dad? Did the ghost of Uncle Abner disturb your sleep?'

'No,' answered her father. 'No ghosts, Abner or otherwise. I slept very well, thank you.'

'This clean, clear air put me out like a light,' said her mother.

'Well now,' her father stood up and waved a spatula in the air, 'are you ready for breakfast? We've almost shrunk away to skin and bones waiting for you, sleepy-head.'

It was a family tradition that her father made breakfast on the weekends. In no time he had bacon, home fries and eggs sizzling on Abner's old iron griddle.

The children were called and they came through the door full of giggles and talk and plans for forts and tree-houses. Trudy had an enormous armful of loosestrife, which Elizabeth arranged in a milk-glass pitcher. The purply pink of the flowers and the white pitcher with reflecting fire at its edges looked especially pretty together.

'You've got a good eye for decorating,' said her mother. 'Too bad you won't have the fun of decorating this charming place.'

'Oh Mom,' Josh looked pained. 'Does that mean we can't stay?'

'I'm afraid it does,' Elizabeth answered as lightly as she could.

Trudy put her elbows on the table and rested her chin in her hands. 'Well, what is Josh supposed to do with Cat then?'

'Shhhhhhhhh,' Josh hissed at his sister.

'Who's Cat?' Elizabeth asked.

'But Josh,' Trudy turned to Josh, 'what are you going to do with him? He can't live all his life in your pocket.'

'What sort of cat do you have in your pocket, Josh?' Elizabeth asked.

'It's not a cat . . .' Trudy began.

'SHHHHHHHH!' hissed Josh.

'I'm afraid it's too late to cover your tracks, old boy.' Elizabeth's father put his arm affectionately around Josh's slim shoulders. 'As the saying goes, Trudy has let the CAT out of the bag.'

'Oh, okay.' Josh frowned and carefully pulled something out of his pocket. Out popped a big round knobbly toad.

'There's Cat,' smiled Trudy. 'Isn't he ugly? I thought his name should be Ugly.'

'Of course that's what everybody would have called him,' Josh explained. 'I didn't think he should have an ordinary name, that's why I named him Cat. And besides, he likes to be skritched just like a cat.'

Josh gently rubbed the toad's side with a grass stalk.

The toad leaned into the scratching and half shut his eyes. He did seem to be enjoying it.

'Can I keep him, Mom?' Josh pleaded.

'Cat likes Josh already,' Trudy added, trying in her best four-year-old way to be helpful.

'Toads don't like apartments in New York very well,' Elizabeth answered. 'They like trees and fresh air and lots of bugs.'

'So do children,' her father put in.

'Boys should have toads, I always say,' added her mother.

Elizabeth looked exasperated. 'You two are a lot of help.'

'We're just trying to get you to look at what you've got here,' said her father.

'An asset,' Elizabeth answered, annoyed.

'Yes dear, that's true, it is a valuable asset. But it's something else, something more. It's a free vacation. You could stay the rest of the summer. The children could enjoy the outdoors without supervision and you could have a quiet place to study. You don't have to be back in the city until school starts. I could send you up your clothes and let you use my station-wagon. It wouldn't hurt to wait to put the place up for sale in the fall.'

'It will sell better in the summer,' Elizabeth said quietly, her voice under strict control.

'Perhaps that's true,' her father replied, 'but this place is loaded with charm. I don't think it will make much difference one way or another. In my opinion it would sell well in a blizzard at twenty below.'

'We really don't want to butt into your business,' said her mother. 'You can always do as you please, Elizabeth. After all, it is your place. You can just say no, dear, and we'll all have to abide by your decision.'

'Can we stay, Mom, can we please?' begged Josh. 'I'll help you sweep and pump the water. I'm strong. I can be lots of help.' Josh cocked his arms to show his seven-year-old muscles.

'Me too, me too!' Trudy added. 'See, I'm strong too!' She cocked her little arms.

Elizabeth shook her head and smiled in spite of herself. 'I will only tell you ALL, that I will think about it — no promises,' she warned.

While doing up the breakfast dishes, Elizabeth tried to think of a way to ask to borrow the car. She wanted to apologize to Stannard. No need to let things end on a bitter note, she told herself again. She had been tired and upset yesterday. She hadn't given him a chance to explain. Finally she just asked — 'Mother, can I borrow your car for an errand?'

'Errands already?' asked her mother. 'Today is Sunday.'

'I know it's Sunday . . . I owe somebody an apology.'

'The young man on the phone?'

'Stannard, Gare Stannard is his name . . . and yes, he's the one.'

'Well, good,' said her mother. 'I was hoping we'd get to meet him.'

'I was planning to go by myself, Mother. It's hard enough to apologize without an audience, you know.'

'Well, yes, dear. I didn't think of that. Of course you go along. Charlie!' she shouted out of the door at her husband, who was out in the yard with the children. 'Give Elizabeth the keys to the car, dear. She needs to borrow it for a little while.'

'Where are you going, Mom?' Josh came running up delivering the keys from his grandfather.

'Down the road,' Elizabeth answered.

'Where down the road?' Josh asked.

'Mommy, are you going to the store?' asked Trudy. 'Can I have an ice-cream?'

'You just had breakfast,' Elizabeth answered. 'And no, I'm not going to the store.'

'Well then, where are you going?' Josh asked in his most grown-up voice.

'I'm going down the road to see someone, that's where I'm going.' One of Elizabeth's cardinal rules was never to lie to the children, but there were times when she was sorely tempted.

'Are you going to see the man with the raccoon?' Josh asked.

'No . . . well, I mean yes . . . well, I don't think he really has a raccoon . . . exactly.'

'He said he had a raccoon, Mom. He told me so on the telephone. Oh, Mom, I never met a real raccoon before. Can I go with you?'

'Me either! Me too! Please, Mommy!' Trudy turned her eyes pleadingly on Elizabeth.

'Oh for goodness sake!' Elizabeth shook her head and laughed. 'All right, we'll all go. I haven't won an argument or a discussion since I got to this state. No sense even trying. Come on. Come on, Mother. Come on, Dad,' she called to her father. 'We're going to see a man about a rac-coon!'

Her father came hurrying up the lawn. 'Oh boy,' he said with a twinkle in his eye. 'I never met a real raccoon before!'

With that, both women burst into laughter.

'What did I say? It wasn't that funny, was it?' asked her father.

'Must run in the family,' said her mother. 'Come on, Charlie, I'll explain it to you later. Let's go see that man about a raccoon.'

When they got to Stannard's drive, Elizabeth began to get cold feet. Maybe this wasn't such a good idea after all. She didn't want Stannard to think she was encouraging him. She most defi-nitely wasn't. She was just about to tell her father to turn around, when Stannard came pushing a lawn-mower around the corner of his house . . . followed by a raccoon.

'Mom! Look! I told you he had a raccoon!' Josh was so excited he couldn't sit still.

Elizabeth felt a strange excitement too rising in her middle. Must be the bacon I had for breakfast, she told herself.

Stannard shut off the noisy mower and smiled hello. The little coon caught up to him and started to climb his pant leg.

'Look, Mommy, the little raccoon thinks that man's a tree!' Trudy giggled.

'Can I pet him?' Josh asked.

Stannard reached down and grabbed the little animal and cradled him in his arms.

Elizabeth had to smile at his gentleness.

Her parents introduced themselves and Josh said — 'I'm Josh,' and put out his hand. 'I'm Trudy,' Trudy said shyly, looking at the ground and twisting one foot.

'Glad to meet you, Trudy and Josh, and the whole family.'

Elizabeth hung back. She didn't greet Stannard. And he didn't greet her beyond a slight nod in her direction.

'Does he have a name?' Josh asked. He hadn't taken his eyes off the coon for a moment.

'No, not that he's told me,' Stannard chuckled.

'Look!' said Trudy, 'he's got green feet!'

'That's from walking in the fresh-cut grass,' Stannard explained. 'Here,' he said to Josh, 'would you like to hold him?'

Josh carefully took the little coon, who immediately climbed out of the boy's arms and onto his shoulders. He churred and burred.

'What's he saying?' Josh asked, trying to crane his neck around to look at his furry living collar.

'He's probably saying he's pleased to make your acquaintance,' Stannard smiled.

'Oh that tickles!' Josh giggled as the little coon ran his paws down inside his shirt. 'What's he looking for in my shirt?' Josh asked.

'Raccoons are one hundred per cent curiosity,' Stannard replied. 'He's not looking for anything in particular. He's just checking out the territory. He wants to see if there might be something hidden in there — a crayfish, or a warm tasty bug, maybe even a cookie.'

'Well,' Josh answered, 'there's nothing in there but me. We don't have any cookies with us, do we, Mom?'

'No,' Elizabeth replied. Her voice cracked and sounded not at all like her own to her ears. She felt her cheeks flush.

'Where did you get him?' Josh asked.

'Your mother found him.' Stannard looked at Elizabeth, his eyes were smiling.

'You did? You found him, Mom? Why didn't you tell us?' Josh asked.

'Well, I didn't exactly find him,' Elizabeth began . . . 'he found me.'

'He followed your mother down the road the other night, when she came to use my phone to call you. Do you remember we were talking about a raccoon?' Stannard asked.

Josh nodded.

'Weren't you scared?' her mother asked.

'Yes, I was,' Elizabeth answered, relieved that her mother had the same reaction that she had had. She didn't feel so foolish now. 'It was almost dark,' she went on, 'and I had no idea what sort of animal was following me.'

Josh had the little coon back in his hands. He held him out at arm's length. 'He's pretty little, Mom. What sort of animal did you think it was?'

'I thought it was a snipe,' Elizabeth admitted.

'A snipe? Elizabeth!' chuckled her father. 'A snipe?'

'You told me that on the phone, I remember,' nodded Josh.

'Your mother,' Stannard continued, 'had been warned by one of our local boys to look out for snipes. It was a natural conclusion for a city gal to come to.'

Elizabeth glared at Stannard. For some reason it made her angry to have Stannard defend her. She would defend herself, thank you. 'How was I to know what a snipe was?' she began with some heat. 'I don't know beans about raccoons, or snipes or skunks and I freely admit it. Ask me about wills and deeds and writs, that's my field.'

'The lady's a lawyer?' asked Stannard.

'Not yet,' Elizabeth shot back, 'but she will be.'

'Hurrah,' said Stannard, 'and more power to her. I like a lady who knows her own mind.'

Elizabeth was surprised by his reaction. She couldn't decide if he meant it as a compliment or a dig. She decided to accept it as a compliment. 'Thank you,' she said simply.

'You're welcome,' Stannard replied. 'Are we declaring a truce here?' he asked.

Her mother and father had strolled a little way off and were admiring the view. Josh and Trudy were following the raccoon, who was loping around the lawn.

'I think so,' she smiled. It felt good to smile. She was tired of being on the defensive. 'I wanted to come and apologize for yesterday,' she went on almost shyly. 'Then everyone wanted to come too.' She waved a hand to include her parents and her children.

'I'm glad they did,' he answered.

'But now I'm not so sure you deserve an apology . . . saying I found the coon and all . . .'

He smiled down at her. 'I accept.'

'But I didn't offer it yet,' she protested.

"That's all right,' he replied. 'With you I'll take what I can get.'

She blushed and didn't know what to say.

'So . . .' he filled the space, 'you're lucky to have such nice parents. Nice kids too.'

'Thank you.'

'Your car will be roadworthy tomorrow . . . I suppose that means you'll be heading on back down-country?' He tried to sound nonchalant but he was watching her face closely. It came as a nice surprise to Elizabeth to see that he really did care about her answer to that question. She noted that something in her cared about it too. She tried to dismiss the tug she was feeling, but she couldn't quite ignore it altogether.

'To tell the truth I haven't made up my mind as yet,' she answered. 'My mom and dad have been trying to talk me into staying the rest of the summer. They'd like to see the children have a summer in the country. And of course the kids are crazy about the place.'

'How about their mother?' He kicked a thistle out of the grass with the toe of his boot. 'How does she feel about the place?'

'I must admit she would have rode out of here

in a cloud of dust just yesterday,' she replied. 'But now . . . well, I guess it's growing on me.'

'Good,' he said.

'Yes, well, I'd have to be deaf and blind not to see how delighted the children are.'

'Great place for kids.'

'Yes, I can see that. But as I also said, I haven't made up my mind to stay for sure . . . yet.'

'I see.' He turned away to watch the children. She couldn't see the expression on his face. She had a mad urge to run around in front of him to see, but of course she didn't. Funny, she thought to herself, why did she care? It was a momentary whim, that's all. He was a nice person. A nice-looking man. Okay, so he was a sexy man. That still didn't make it really matter what Gare Stannard thought about her plans to stay or not to stay . . . did it?

When all the goodbyes had been said, they pulled out of Stannard's yard. Stannard picked up the little coon and waved his paw goodbye to the children.

'Look, Mommy, the little raccoon is waving 'bye just like a baby person.' Trudy waved first one hand, then the other, then both.

'I hope we can stay here, Mom,' Josh said seriously. 'I would like to be able to play with that raccoon again.'

'I like Mr Stannard,' said Trudy. 'He's nice. Maybe we should marry him.'

Elizabeth's mother and father both choked back laughter at that suggestion. Elizabeth, her-

78

self, couldn't help grinning.

'Well,' said the little girl, hurt that the grown-ups were laughing at what seemed to her a perfectly sound suggestion, 'I like him!'

'So do I.' Elizabeth hugged her daughter.

'I do too,' said her grandmother.

'He's a good old shoe,' said her grandfather.

'What's a good old shoe?' asked Trudy.

'That means your grandfather likes him too,' Elizabeth smiled.

She leaned back and watched the trees and meadows slide by the window. Marry Stannard? Even if she did decide to stay in Vermont for the rest of the summer, she certainly had no intention of staying that long. Marry Stannard? No way. She was a city girl. He was right about that. Her life was in the city. A couple more years of schooling, pass the bar exam, and then into the prestigious firm of McCracken, McCracken and Town — Ted's old firm. McCracken senior had already promised her a place when she was ready. It was a dream come true, much too good to be thrown away for a quick summer romance that got out of hand. If she stayed, she'd have to be careful not to let the sexy Mr Stannard get too close and ruin her career, her plans and her life.

Seven

They were halfway through a very silent breakfast the next morning before Elizabeth made her announcement. 'I can't stand these long faces,' she began, trying to keep a straight and sombre face herself. Trudy was stirring her cereal. 'Even though I know you will all have strong reactions to my decision . . .' She paused and looked around the table. Josh let out a long and hopeless sigh. 'I've decided,' she continued, 'to stay the summer.'

Josh's eyes grew bigger and bigger as he took in the news.

'Hurrah! Hooray!' the children cheered.

'Three cheers for Mom!' whooped her father. 'Hip-hip-hooray — yeah Mom!' he led the children with great delight. Even her mother, who was usually quite ladylike, joined in.

After finishing breakfast to the accompaniment of the noisy excitement of the children, Elizabeth and her father rode into Bridgeton to retrieve the station-wagon.

'I'm Elizabeth Elkins,' Elizabeth announced to the sandy-haired attendant at Tommy's Garage. 'Are you Tommy?'

'None other,' he grinned. 'So, you are Elizabeth!' He looked her up and down. Elizabeth blushed. 'Gare still has the touch. He can pick a winner every time,' he chuckled.

Elizabeth bristled. 'I'll thank you to keep your opinions to yourself. Is my car ready?'

'And the lady's spirited to boot.' Tommy continued to smile while wiping his hands on a rag he kept in his back pocket. 'Yes, Elizabeth Elkins, your car is ready.'

'What do I owe you?' Elizabeth asked, her voice as icy as she could make it.

'Let's see.' Tommy thumbed through a helter-skelter pile of yellow sheets he had clipped inside a metal notebook. 'Here it is!' He handed her a grease-smudged sheet. 'No extra charge for my personal fingerprints,' he grinned. 'That's artistic interpretation,' he added.

Elizabeth was quite pleased with the amount. She had expected an enormous charge. This was quite modest. She relaxed her frown. She couldn't continue to be angry at an auto mechanic who charged fairly. He was a rarity, she decided, and entitled to some zaniness. She wrote him out a cheque and handed it over. 'Thank you.'

'You're welcome.' He clicked his heels and did a little salute. 'Have a safe trip home.'

'Thank you.' She was walking toward the old station-wagon and had to turn to talk back over her shoulder. 'But we aren't going just yet.'

'Oh?' He raised his eyebrows.

She climbed into the familiar old wagon and turned it on. The motor seemed to run more smoothly than she remembered.

'I touched up the carburettor a bit,' Tommy

was nodding, his head cocked to one side listening to the engine. 'Runs better, don't you think?'

'Yes,' Elizabeth agreed. 'Thank you again. I appreciate all you've done.'

'That's okay,' Tommy waved away her thanks. 'I'm partial to motors. You take care of them, they'll take care of you. Simple. Say hello to Gare for me. He's a good old boy,' he added.

'I will,' she promised.

As she followed her father first to the store and then back to Abner's, she wondered just when she would see that good old boy Gare again. He didn't know she had decided to stay in Vermont. As far as he knew, last evening was the last he'd ever see of her. She wondered how she could let him know she was still around and not seem obvious about it.

Now Elizabeth, she told herself, you have piles of studying to do. No need to get all gaga over a nice neighbour. Leave well enough alone. But she kept trying to think of a reasonable reason to drop in on her nice neighbour. 'I know!' she said aloud, pleased with herself. 'I'll wait a day or so and ask to use his phone to call my parents!' She planned to have a phone installed, but surely that wouldn't happen for several days. Using the phone was a good plausible excuse to drop in on Mr Gare Stannard.

Her mother and father left just after lunch. Elizabeth watched their car disappear from sight and sighed. The children were playing tag, making great circles around the house. To stay certainly was the right decision for them, she reflected. She hoped it would prove to be right for herself.

Late in the afternoon she heard a car pull into the yard. She looked up from the textbook on the table and was surprised to see a blue fender through the half-open door. Her heart leapt. That surprised her too. 'Down, girl,' she whispered to herself. There are all sorts of blue cars and trucks in the world. Besides that, even if it was that particular blue pick-up, there was no need to get all gooey-eyed about its owner. What was there about Gare Stannard anyway? He was just an ordinary man, maybe a little better looking than average, but really just ordinary.

She got up and went to the door. It was Stannard. The look of him, tall and muscular, standing beside his blue pick-up smiling around the pipe in his mouth at her children, brought a smile to her lips.

He caught sight of her in the doorway. He took his pipe out of his mouth and raised it in hello. 'Hi, Mom.'

'Mommy,' Josh called, 'come see what Gare has in his truck.'

'Gare says it's a "turnable duck",' Trudy giggled.

'Mr Stannard, not Gare,' she instructed the children, as she walked out to the pick-up.

'That's my fault,' Gare apologized. 'I told them to call me Gare. I hope you don't mind?'

83

He regarded her with an even, open gaze.

'No,' she replied and looked away from those eyes. It's dangerous to look too long into eyes, she reminded herself. 'Now, what is this about?' she changed the subject.

'A returnable duck named Reina,' Gare chuckled and nodded toward the penned white duck in the back of his truck.

'Gawhack!' quacked the duck, standing up and flapping her wings.

'Does she know her name?' Josh asked.

'Maybe,' Gare answered. 'With a duck it's hard to know. When she's in the mood, she might.'

'What's a "returnable duck"?' Elizabeth asked.

'A duck that goes back to its owners when they return from vacation,' Gare explained. 'I'm duck-sitting.'

Elizabeth laughed. 'A duck-sitter, that's certainly different.'

'Yep,' he chuckled, 'folks just call me the critter-sitter.'

'Critter-sitter,' she laughed.

'So, you've decided to stay, I hear,' he smiled at her.

'Where did you hear that?' she asked, surprised. 'Tommy?'

'Yes, Tommy told me when I stopped for gas. And Mrs Clemons at the store said she thought maybe you might be staying on a while. She said you bought a pile of groceries.'

'Holy cow! What else did you hear?' She didn't know whether she should be flattered or alarmed.

'Oh,' Gare continued offhandedly, 'Tommy said he got your dander up, but you calmed down after a while. He said you were pretty.'

'He did, did he.'

'Yes, and he said he'd be careful of city gals, if he were me. He said things just get interesting and they leave.'

'That's what he said?' Elizabeth couldn't believe that her presence had elicited so much notice and talk.

'This is the country, you know.' Gare knocked the ashes out of his pipe against the heel of his boot. 'Country people notice other people. They say if you're a fugitive from the law, you should never come to the country. You'll stick out like a sore thumb. If you want to disappear from view, go to the city, get lost in the crowd. Interesting, isn't it?'

'Hmmmm yes, I guess so.' Elizabeth was still worrying about the talk of her presence. 'I don't know that I like being talked about.'

'They mean no harm,' Gare replied. 'It's just country ways. If you stay around long enough, you'll see for yourself.'

'Well perhaps,' Elizabeth allowed.

'Gare?' Josh jumped into the pause in their conversation.

'Yes, Josh?'

'Can the duck come out and play with us? I

mean, can you let her out here?'

'If your Mom approves.' He looked at Elizabeth for permission.

'I don't know anything about ducks,' Elizabeth replied. 'I'll rely on Mr Stannard's good judgement.'

'Please call me Gare,' he said, unlatching the pen and scooping up the squawking duck.

'Why is she squawking, Gare?' Trudy looked alarmed.

'Because she's a duck,' Gare answered. He put the duck down on the ground. She spread her wings and ran squawking loudly down the lawn.

'What's she saying?' Josh asked.

'What do you think?' Gare asked in return.

'She sounds mad to me,' Josh answered. 'I think she's yelling at us.'

'I think you're right,' Gare laughed. 'I think she thinks she's queen of the ducks. Maybe even queen of the world. Ducks are very full of self-importance. She's probably yelling about our poor manners in the presence of Her Royal Majesty the Quacker Queen.'

Josh giggled. 'The Quacker Queen, that's funny.'

The children took off down the lawn after the duck with arms outstretched, mimicking the quack-quack as they went.

'Would you like to keep the duck for the summer?' Gare asked.

'What do I want with a duck?' Elizabeth questioned, quite taken aback.

'It was just a friendly suggestion,' Gare replied. 'I thought the kids would get a bang out of a "turnable duck". She's little problem really. I've got a bag of feed for her, her pen and her dish-pan.'

'Dish-pan? What does she do, cook her own meals?'

'No,' laughed Stannard. 'The dish-pan is her pond. Fill it up with water and she'll sit in it for hours. She's a family pet. She grew up with dogs and cats and children. I doubt she realizes that she's a duck. As a matter of fact she's afraid of any body of water larger than her dish-pan.'

Elizabeth laughed. 'Now that really is funny.'

'I guarantee she'll entertain you. If she gives you any trouble, I'll take her back. I just thought you and the children might enjoy her antics. You only have to fill her dish-pan and feed her and round her up if you're going to be away, and at night.'

'Round her up?'

'Yes, well, she'll come to be fed, but she'd rather not go in her pen. So you have to catch her and put her in.'

'Does she peck?'

'No, she just complains loudly. Grab her around her middle. It's not hard.'

'Why pen her if she doesn't like it?'

'She'd make a tasty dinner for a fox,' he answered.

'I see,' Elizabeth nodded her head. She watched her children giggling over the duck-chase up and down the lawn. 'Well, I guess we can give it a try.'

The children were delighted to hear that Reina the 'turnable duck' would be staying with them for the summer.

'We've got a real pet now,' Josh announced. He had the toad, Cat, in a terrarium in his room. But a real pet didn't sit quietly in a terrarium gulping down flies. According to Josh, a real pet could play with you.

They soon fell into an easy system for their country summer days. The children would eat breakfast and go outdoors to play, while Elizabeth would hit the books. She'd see them again at lunch unless they made sandwiches and had a picnic down by the meadow brook. Sometimes she would give herself permission to go with them.

Reina Duck would waddle after the children down the grassy path to the tiny stream that meandered through the meadow. Trudy and Josh laboured for days on end making dams and sluiceways of stones and sticks. Reina would sit on the bank and sleep or quack warnings at them for playing in what to her were dangerous amounts of water.

The children made nice little ponds and would quietly soothe Reina's feathers and put her into the small patches of water. Reina would have none of it. She would squawk and gulp and dash to the safety of the bank and scold them loudly in outraged duck.

Stannard stopped by almost every evening. Sometimes he took the children down to his house to visit the raccoon. He brought them scraps of wood to make sailing-ships. And he showed them how to make a simple water-wheel. And he always sat and talked to Elizabeth about the things that two people, who are friends, talk about at the end of the day. Once in a while Elizabeth would invite him to stay and eat with them. Sometimes he did.

He called Elizabeth — Cassie or Mom. Elizabeth tried to make him change his mind about her name. 'You're exasperating, do you know that?' she said one evening over grilled chicken.

'How's that?' he raised his eyebrows.

'My name is Elizabeth but you steadfastly refuse to call me Elizabeth.'

'Yes?'

'I have a right to my name, don't you agree?'

He licked his fingers. 'This barbeque sauce is too good to waste,' he said.

'I have a right to be called by any name I choose, don't you agree?' she persisted.

'I suppose so,' he nodded.

'Then, why won't you call me Elizabeth?'

'I told you already,' he answered simply, 'I don't think it fits you.'

'Cassius Clay got the whole world to call him by the name he chose. A whole world of sportscasters and fans now call him Muhammad Ali. Why can't I be Elizabeth to you — one person?'

'Tell you what,' his eyes twinkled, 'when you become heavyweight boxing champ of the world, I'll call you Muhammad Ali.'

'AAAAugh!' Elizabeth grumped. She threw up her hands. 'I give up!'

'Good,' he grinned. 'You've got barbeque sauce on your nose.'

One evening it was pouring rain. It had been damp and chilly all day. When Stannard stopped by, he found the little family wrapped in sweaters and still cold. 'Why don't you build a fire in the stove?' he asked.

'I don't know anything about stoves,' Elizabeth replied. 'I was afraid I'd burn the house down.'

'Come on, let's get some wood out of the woodshed and have a lesson in stove tending.'

In no time he had a cheery fire crackling away in the old cast-iron stove.

'It smells good in here.' Josh sniffed the air.

'I like this.' Trudy hugged herself. 'I feel toasty already.'

'We should stay here all the time,' said Josh. 'Now that we know how to keep ourselves warm, we could stay all winter.'

'No way, Josh,' Elizabeth smiled at her son. 'Don't go getting any fancy ideas. This is just a summer vacation. It's not a permanent thing.'

'Ahhh, Mom,' Josh replied. 'I thought you liked it here. The other day you said you did.'

'I do,' Elizabeth answered. 'It's a wonderful place to spend the summer.'

Stannard had been tipped back in his chair, smoking his pipe and listening to mother and son. 'He's right, you know, you could stay.'

'Right!' said Elizabeth with some heat. 'I have enough trouble with my children wanting to stay. Don't you start too. I do not intend to give up my schooling and my career because this is a nice vacation spot. I've waited too long for this. I've put in too much time. And besides that, I like the law. I want to be a lawyer . . . and I intend to be!' She felt like crying. 'I don't see why I should have to argue and fight with my family about this . . .' She stopped. She knew if she went on, she'd be in tears.

'Whoops,' said Stannard. His chair slipped out from under him and he had to do some fancy footwork to keep from falling.

'You shouldn't tip back in your chair,' said Trudy.

'You're right, Trudy,' Stannard answered the child seriously. 'I shouldn't do that. It's a bad habit. If you see me tipping my chair, you remind me, okay?'

'Okay,' she answered brightly.

'Bedtime, you two.' Elizabeth glanced at her wristwatch. 'Hurry on up and get into your pyjamas. I'll be up to tuck you in. Say goodnight to Gare.'

'Goodnight, Gare.' Josh came over and shook hands. 'Thank you for showing us how to make a fire in the stove . . . even if we can't stay all winter.'

'Goodnight, Gare,' said Trudy. She threw her arms around his neck and gave him a hug. As the little girl disappeared up the stairs, they heard her ask her brother — 'Is Gare our father?'

'No,' Josh answered, 'he's only our almost father.'

Elizabeth blushed.

Gare came up softly behind her. 'I could be . . . Cassie?'

She turned and looked up into his questioning eyes. He bent slightly and kissed her gently.

'Mom?' Josh was halfway back down the stairs watching them.

Elizabeth turned quickly from Stannard, embarrassed. Josh didn't seem to be bothered in the least. 'What?' she asked in a shaky voice.

'Should I wear my blue pyjamas tonight? They're warmer.'

'Yes,' she answered, 'wear the blue ones.'

'Okay,' he said cheerily and went back upstairs.

'Cassie . . . ?' Gare put a hand around her waist and drew her to him again. She let herself be enveloped in his arms. It felt so warm, so good, so like home. They kissed and Elizabeth felt the power of the electricity they created burn down to her toes.

'No, no,' she pulled back and away. 'No, I don't want to want you like this.'

'But, Cassie . . .'

'No, I don't want to need you, don't you understand? I don't want to need you this way . . .

and I will. I won't give up my dream. I've waited too long,' she sobbed.

'Go to school here,' he said.

'Don't you understand?' she asked again. 'I want it written on my tombstone that I was a lawyer, that I did something special in my life.'

'Raising kids is special,' he said.

'Yes, yes, but I want more.'

'Having your kids grow up to be nice people, that's important.'

'I know, I know,' she answered miserably. 'You once said your great-grandmother Stannard knew what she wanted. Well, I know what I want. And just because it's not what my mother or father or you want me to want, doesn't mean I don't want it. I have that right.'

'You do indeed,' he agreed. 'But why can't you go to school here?'

'Where here?'

'Here in Vermont.'

'The university is too far from here. It wouldn't work.'

'Not the university.'

'Where then, Tommy's Garage?' she asked sarcastically.

'No, the Vermont Law School.'

'You're making that up.'

'No, I'm not. The Vermont Law School is only twenty minutes away . . . cross my heart.'

Eight

The very next evening Gare brought her a Vermont Law School catalogue. 'See here, Lady lawyer, the Vermont Law School does exist and furthermore it's in West Royalston, only fifteen miles from the end of your driveway. I clocked it.'

'Well, what do you know,' she smiled a half smile at him. 'Thank you.' She appreciated what he was trying to do. But some dinky little law school in the wilds of Vermont certainly couldn't hold a candle to Columbia University in the city. No, she had worked long and hard to get into the best and that's where she wanted to be. She wouldn't go into that right now. She'd break the news to him more gently over a period of time.

'What smells so good in here?' he asked. 'Don't tell me lady lawyers bake too,' he teased.

'Oh you,' she swatted him playfully. 'I was looking through a file of Abner's recipes this morning. Some of them were well-nigh unreadable, they have been used and splattered so much. One of the worst-looking ones was for honey bread, so I thought I'd give it a try.'

'Ah-ha, a bit of the detective in you too,' he grinned. 'If it tastes half as good as it smells, I'd say you've unearthed a winner.'

'Would you care to stay and try it?' she invited.

'I wish I could but I've got to make a speech tonight at the Cornwall Fortnightly Club. It's an area woman's club. They're interested in doing some conservation projects. It's part of my job to inform the public — especially when they ask.'

'Hmmmm,' she answered. 'Woman's club?' She imagined a roomful of sexy young women fluttering around the handsome Mr Stannard.

And as though he had read her mind, he answered, 'Yep, all those pretty gals just waiting to get their hands on me.'

'Oh you!' she swatted him again.

'Yes, indeed,' he grinned. 'Why, I'll bet there's not one under sixty in the whole bunch.'

'Oh you!' She took after him again.

'Down-down-down,' he laughed. 'Whew! Lady lawyers certainly are hard to get along with. I'd better get out of here while I'm still standing. See you tomorrow.' He was out of the door and Elizabeth was laughing, but she was sorry to see him go. He was becoming very much a part of her life. Careful, she told herself. Careful.

'Mommy?' Josh came barging in from outside. 'Can I ride home with Gare? I want to see the raccoon. I can walk back home. It's still light enough. Gare says he thinks it's safe and I'm old enough. Can I, Mom? Can I?'

'Oh all right,' she answered. 'But don't dawdle on the way home. Come straight away, hear?' She was getting used to the safety of the country. And she was also getting used to letting Gare have some say over the children. It just seemed natural. It also seemed very nice. It was a pleasure to have someone to share the responsibilities and joys of parenthood with.

Not more than twenty minutes passed when the phone rang. 'Cassie — Gare here. I just waved Josh goodbye. He looked a little doubtful but I assured him he was old enough and brave enough to make it home on his own. He'll probably come flying in your door in about ten minutes, having run all the way.' She could hear the smile in his voice. 'Just wanted to tell you so you'd know when to expect him.'

'Thanks so much. I appreciate your call. You're off to see the ladies, I suppose?'

'Yep, lucky me.'

Elizabeth felt a twinge. She wasn't jealous. Of course she wasn't. 'Thanks again,' she repeated.

'You're welcome again. Wish me luck.'

'Yeah, all kinds of luck,' she said lamely.

'What?' he asked. 'Do I detect a hint of jealousy?'

'No, I'm not jealous. I haven't a jealous bone in my body,' she shot back. 'Besides that, I have no claim on you, Mr Stannard. You're a completely free man as far as I'm concerned.'

'Ah, that's what I was afraid of,' he replied half-jokingly. 'Well, see you tomorrow if I make it through tonight.'

When Elizabeth hung up the phone, she was aware of an uncomfortable feeling somewhere in the vicinity of her stomach . . . or was it her throat . . . or the bridge of her nose? I'm probably coming down with something, she grumbled under her breath.

Just as Stannard had predicted, in ten minutes time Josh came sprinting through the door. 'Hi, Mom!' he gasped. 'It was easy,' he panted. 'See, I told you I was almost grown up,' he announced proudly.

Elizabeth gave her son a hug.

'Ahhh, Mom, do you have to do that?' he squirmed. 'Men don't like all that mushy stuff. That's girl's stuff.'

'I wouldn't be too sure about that if I were you,' Elizabeth grinned. 'There may be a few things you've yet to discover about being a man.'

'Oh, Mom.' Josh gave his mother an exasperated look. 'Gare says I'm getting old enough and brave. He's a man, so he knows all about it,' Josh went on in his seven-year-old logic.

'Yes, I suppose he does.' Elizabeth raised her eyebrows. In her view Gare Stannard knew entirely too much about how to be an enticing male.

'What's that?' Josh asked. A soft scratching sound was coming from the screen door. Elizabeth and Josh both turned to look. A tiny black hand curled around the edge of the door. As they watched wide-eyed, the door opened and in walked the raccoon, burring loudly.

'Coonish!' Josh laughed. 'You bad boy. You followed me home!'

The little half-grown coon came straight over to the boy and wanted to be picked up. Josh picked him up and he churred his pleasure.

'Joshua?' Elizabeth asked, her tone of voice asking the obvious question.

'Mom, I didn't do anything. Honest. Gare says Coonish is getting far too smart for his own good. He must have undone the latch on his cage. Can I feed him a cracker, Mom?'

Elizabeth smiled weakly. 'I suppose so,' she sighed. She had no idea how to have a raccoon for a houseguest. She wondered how long that woman's club meeting would last. What if someone enticed Gare to stay longer and chat over coffee and cake? That would probably be the natural order of things. She could just see some sweet young thing taking advantage of the situation to work her charms on him. Elizabeth really didn't like the idea of Gare and a roomful of women. She didn't like to admit it even to herself and certainly never to him, but she was just the tiniest bit jealous . . . for no good reason. She had no claim on him and wanted no claim on him. It was illogical to be jealous, but there it was, she was . . . somewhat . . . a little . . . very little of course.

The little coon was content to let Josh hold him while he ate the cracker, but when it was gone, he wanted to get down.

Trudy came down from upstairs just then. When she spied the raccoon, she clapped her hands. 'Oh, the raccoon!' she grinned. 'Did Gare give him to you?' she asked her brother.

'No,' he answered. 'Coonish followed me home.'

'Mommy, can we keep him?' Trudy asked.

'No,' her brother answered. 'We can't keep him.'

'Why not?'

'Because Gare said so,' Josh replied. 'I asked.'

Whew, Elizabeth thought to herself.

Josh had put the raccoon on the floor and he was busily investigating all corners of the room. When he started to take his investigation into the living-room, Elizabeth shut the doors.

The raccoon was soon satisfied that he had checked all corners of the kitchen. He stood up on his haunches and fiddled with the latch on a lower cupboard. His clever little hands seemed to have minds of their own. While the raccoon looked around from side to side, his little hand-like paws were solving the problem of how the latch worked. Before Josh could catch him, he had the cupboard door unlatched and in he went.

'Oh my gosh!' said Elizabeth.

'See, Mom, I told you he was clever.'

'Yes, very,' Elizabeth admitted drily. 'Catch him, can you . . . before he breaks something.'

Josh got down on his hands and knees and peered into the cupboard.

'Hissss, snap,' went the raccoon.

Josh pulled his head back out. 'He doesn't want to come out.'

'Try again . . . carefully,' Elizabeth urged.

Josh put his head back inside the cupboard.

'Hissss, snap,' went the raccoon.

'Nope,' said Josh, reappearing. 'It makes him mad. I think we'll have to wait until he's through looking around.'

The raccoon was in no hurry to complete his survey of the inside of the cupboard. 'Clankity, clank!' The pots and pans told of his progress, then one of the drawers bumped and jiggled.

'He's in the drawer,' Trudy giggled.

Josh tried to open the drawer but it wouldn't budge. He looked back inside the cupboard. 'He's hanging off the back of the drawer,' he laughed.

'Skidderity-clang,' they could hear the silverware being pushed around inside the drawer.

'Maybe he wants to eat with a spoon,' Trudy suggested.

'Not in my house,' Elizabeth answered, but she couldn't help but laugh.

Finally after a complete kitchen investigation and half a dozen crackers, the little coon was content to snuggle up to sleep in Josh's lap.

Elizabeth began calling Gare's number at nine. It wasn't until quarter to ten that he answered.

'I was beginning to think you had gone home with one of your over-sixty ladies,' she quipped.

'Would that bother you?' he asked.

'Not at all,' she replied. 'It's just we have a member of your household down here and I thought you'd like to retrieve him.'

'A member of my household?' he asked. Then before she could answer — 'Let me guess,' he chuckled, 'the coon?'

'Yes. The children were delighted, but I must say you should work on his manners — they're abominable!'

'I can imagine,' he laughed. 'Give me a minute to load the cage in the truck. I'll be right down.'

After Gare arrived and all the stories of the evening told, Elizabeth sent the sleepy children up to get ready for bed.

'Can Gare tuck me in?' Trudy asked.

'Me too?' Josh asked shyly. Even though he was getting to feel he was too old to be tucked in every night, he didn't want to miss out.

Gare looked at her for permission.

She nodded her consent. A small voice of caution spoke up in her head — be careful, Elizabeth, you're letting him further in — too far in — maybe. She dismissed it. Everything would work out. Now was now. It was summer in Vermont. Come fall, everything would be back to normal. It was quite all right to indulge the children in this request.

When Gare came back downstairs, he grinned at her. 'Now, is there anyone else in this house who needs to be tucked in?'

She blushed and felt a quickening shiver prickle her body. 'No-no-no, Mr Stannard,' she used her best school-teacher voice, 'enough is enough. You've done your duty.'

'I was thinking more in terms of pleasure,' he answered softly.

Elizabeth looked down at the floor. She didn't

know what to answer him.

Gare cleared his throat and changed the subject. 'Have you had a chance to look at the Law School catalogue?'

'No,' she answered, 'I haven't. I might as well tell you that I don't really think I'm interested in a Vermont law school. I've been attending Columbia. It's very good. One of the best.' She smiled weakly at his listening face, hoping to cushion the blow somewhat. She didn't want to hurt his feelings. 'I'd hate to change horses in midstream . . . that sort of thing,' she added lamely.

'Doesn't the law require you to look at all the evidence impartially?' he asked.

'Yes, but . . .'

'At least look . . . will you do that? Lawyers should never make decisions being ignorant of the facts, isn't that true?'

'I'll look, I promise, I'll look,' she laughed lightly, trying to take some of the seriousness out of his face.

'Good, good.' He seemed pleased. He relaxed and yawned. 'Excuse me,' he smiled.

She yawned too. 'It's catching.' They both laughed.

Gare glanced at his watch. 'Time for this buckaroo to hit the road and take my wandering critter home.' He tipped an imaginary hat at her and looked directly into her eyes.

She knew what his eyes were asking. She looked away and pretended to have missed the message.

'Night, Cassie,' he called softly back over his shoulder.

'Oh for goodness sake — Elizabeth,' she laughed good-naturedly. 'Elizabeth, Elizabeth, Elizabeth,' she repeated quietly to herself as she watched the blue pick-up leave the yard.

The next morning she read the Vermont Law School catalogue as she had promised. They specialized in environmental law. Well, Gare Stannard certainly was right about having all the facts. Now she could easily say she couldn't consider going to school in Vermont. Environmental law wasn't her field.

That afternoon she took the children into West Royalston to get some new sneakers. She drove by the law school campus, what there was of it — a clutch of old Victorian buildings at one end of the village green. Now, she could even tell Stannard she had gone to look at it. That should settle that problem once and for all.

She bought the children sneakers and then a treat of ice-cream cones from an old-fashioned soda-fountain. They strolled along the main street of West Royalston enjoying their ice-cream and looking in the store windows.

A real-estate sign caught her eye. She left the children on the front steps of the real-estate office to finish their cones, while she went in to put the farm on the market.

'What's a real-estate agent, Mom?' Josh asked when she came out a little later. Having a first-grader who could read on a fifth-grade level wasn't always a good thing, Elizabeth reflected.

'It means people who buy and sell property,' she answered.

'Like selling the farm?' Josh asked, figuring it out immediately.

'Yes, Josh . . . like selling the farm.' She felt like the wicked witch telling him that.

'Oh Mom,' his eyes filled with tears. 'I thought you were getting to love the farm. Mom?'

'I don't want to leave.' Trudy began to cry too, tears mixing with the ice-cream on her face.

The two children stood there crying as though their hearts were broken. People passing by gave Elizabeth long looks. 'Oh for goodness sake, you two . . . stop this . . . you can't always have what you love . . .' She stopped in mid-sentence, listening to her own words echoing in her mind. You can't always have what you love . . . was that true?

She finally managed to get the children to stop crying. Three glum faces walked back to the station-wagon and headed home. When they pulled in the driveway, the little coon came running out to meet them.

'Coonish!' cried Trudy and Josh in unison.

'Maybe he thinks he lives at our house now,' Trudy suggested.

When Josh opened the car door, the coon climbed in and began immediately to check out the bags of groceries in the car.

'Get him out of there!' shouted Elizabeth.

'Hissss, spit,' said the coon.

'He doesn't want to come,' Josh reported. 'I think he thinks he owns that food.' Josh then tried to lure the little coon out of the groceries by offering him chocolate cookies. 'Come on, Coonish,' Josh coaxed. 'These are really real good.'

The coon looked at the grocery bags, then he sniffed the chocolate cookies, then back at the grocery bags, as though he was deciding which might taste better. He finally decided to go with the chocolate cookies. 'Okay, Mom, come get the bags quick!' Josh shouted.

Elizabeth ran the grocery bags into the house, while Josh fed the coon that last of the chocolate cookies. It was becoming all too apparent why the coon's former owners had dumped him in the woods to fend for himself.

Elizabeth ended up throwing out a chewed-into box of cereal, and two tomatoes and three bananas all with large bite-holes.

The groceries were no more than put away when the phone rang. It was Shelley Wood, the real-estate agent. 'I know this is very short notice, Mrs Elkins. But a customer just walked into my office and started describing what he wanted. I couldn't believe my ears,' she said excitedly. 'It sounded just like your place. I told him I had just listed exactly what he was looking for not thirty minutes ago! I was wondering if it would be all right with you to bring him out. He's from out-of-state and only plans to be around here today.'

Elizabeth felt a sinking sensation. She hadn't expected things to happen so soon. She wasn't ready to sell this quickly. Summer wasn't over. Well, surely that could be worked out . . . if someone really wanted the place. She told Shelley to come ahead.

She hung up the phone and fished the chewed cereal box out of the trash and took it outside and handed it to Josh. 'Here, take your hungry fuzzy friend out back someplace away from the house and stuff him with this.'

'Why, Mom?'

'Because someone is coming to look at the house and he doesn't need to know we've been invaded by a nasty-tempered raccoon, that's why.'

'Oh, Mom, he might like raccoons.'

'Yeah, we can ask him,' said Trudy.

'No, you will not ask him,' Elizabeth stated positively.

'But Mommmy . . .'

'No but Mommy about it . . . no coon, no questions. Is that clear?'

Both children nodded solemnly.

Elizabeth walked back up to the house wondering if she had a wart on her nose yet. All wicked witches, after all, had warty noses.

There was just enough time to straighten up a bit before Shelley Wood pulled in the drive with a sleek black car following behind.

The customer's name was Benedict Crowley.

He was full-faced and full-bodied with little eyes that shot quickly around each room, taking everything in with the speed of a pinball machine. He rolled an unlighted cigar around in his mouth. 'Trying to stop smoking,' he chuckled at himself. 'I've ruined more good cigars treating them as pacifiers.'

When he had seen all the rooms, he took a quick stroll around the outside; Shelley and Elizabeth waited by the kitchen door.

When Crowley was halfway around the back, the little coon took it into his head to go meet him. 'Get out of my way!' Crowley's foot quite expertly lifted the little coon and sent him sailing through the air. He landed hard and lay still.

'You've killed him!' shouted Trudy. She was ready to attack Crowley. Josh held her by the back of her shirt.

'No, look Trudy. He's all right.' The coon was sitting up and shaking his head.

'Your coon, kids?' asked Crowley. 'You shouldn't let him bother people.' He rolled his cigar to the other side of his mouth and continued his tour around the house.

Coonish got up and walked over to the children. 'Burrr?' He looked up at them, as if to ask — did I do something wrong?

'Great place.' Crowley completed his circle.

'I won't sell it to someone who wants to change it,' Elizabeth stated. 'I hope Shelley made that clear.'

'Yes, yes she did,' Crowley replied. 'I

wouldn't change a thing. Charming place. Needs work though. In light of that,' Crowley continued, 'I'm willing to offer you . . .' he named an amount somewhat lower than Elizabeth had hoped to get.

'I'll have to think about it,' Elizabeth replied.

'Of course, of course,' Crowley nodded enthusiastically. 'Talk it over with your husband and let me know.'

Elizabeth didn't tell him she had no husband. For the moment, having to talk it over with her husband bought her some time. She was ready to sell. She wanted to sell. It wasn't a bad offer. But she didn't want it to happen all in one day. She just needed a little breathing-space to get used to the idea, that was all.

'Don't take too long deciding,' Crowley smiled around his cigar. 'I get very jittery about people who drag their feet making decisions. I believe you either do a thing or don't. None of this pussyfootin' around business for Benedict Crowley!'

Crowley shook Elizabeth's hand and walked to his fancy car. 'Keep in touch, Mrs Elkins. Let Shelley here know your decision as soon as possible. I'm sure you won't take too long.' He smiled. 'I've made you a good offer.' With that, he got in his car and sped down the road in a cloud of dust.

Shelley rolled her eyes. 'He's quite something, isn't he?'

'Yes,' Elizabeth nodded. 'Though, somehow

he doesn't seem right for this place.'

'Yes, well, I've been in this business long enough to know that you never can tell who will like what. Maybe his wife is crazy about Early American.'

'Maybe,' Elizabeth answered thoughtfully.

'Do you think you'll know what you want to do by next Monday?'

'I'll try,' Elizabeth answered.

Elizabeth was making a stew when she heard Gare's truck pull into the yard. Next she heard the excited voices of the children. Then strangely, things got quiet. She looked out. Gare and the children were standing at the back of the truck. If anyone was talking, they were doing it too low for her to hear.

She continued with her stew preparations and just as she was thinking perhaps she should go see what was going on, they all came in the house. Josh and Trudy looked very glum. Even Gare looked somewhat dampened in spirit. 'We have something to tell you, Mom,' Gare said.

'Josh did something bad,' Trudy offered.

'Trudy! Let me tell it!' Josh said fiercely. 'I put nails behind that mean man's car . . . because he kicked Coonish . . . but he didn't hit them . . . Gare did.' The boy finished in tears.

'Joshua,' said Elizabeth, 'I'm shocked. I never would have thought you'd do a thing like that!'

'I know, I know,' sobbed the boy.

'That's a terrible thing to do. If Mr Crowley

had hit those nails, he might have lost control of his car and crashed. You might have killed him, Josh. Do you understand what I'm saying?'

'Y . . . Y . . . Yes, Mom. Gare told me too.'

'I think we covered the possibilities,' said Gare. 'I think I even have a few handy jobs he can do for me to pay for the damage to my tyre . . . if that's all right with you, that is.'

'Yes, of course,' Elizabeth answered. 'I wonder if he shouldn't go up to bed right now?' Elizabeth looked the question at Gare.

'I have an alternate suggestion . . .' Gare watched her face to see if he had permission to continue. She nodded. 'How would it be if he got ready for bed now, ate his dinner and then went to bed? Not eating is pretty hard on a guy.'

'You're probably right,' Elizabeth answered. 'Lucky for you, young man,' she shook her finger at Josh, 'that you've got such a good lawyer to plead your case. Now scoot!'

Josh ran up the stairs two at a time.

'Are you mad at me too?' asked Trudy, wide-eyed.

'Did you put any nails in the driveway?' asked Elizabeth.

'No, Mommy, I didn't.' The little girl shook her head. 'I was just standing and watching.'

'Did you tell Josh not to do it?' Elizabeth asked.

'No,' . . . she frowned in thought. 'He didn't ask me.'

Gare smothered a grin behind a yawn.

'Next time you see Josh doing something bad, you tell him not to do it . . . even if he doesn't ask. Okay?'

'Okay, Mommy. Can I get my 'jamas on too?'

'Yes,' Elizabeth sighed. 'Go ahead.'

Elizabeth went to check on her stew.

'I've got Coonish in a cage on my truck, in case you're wondering where your unwelcome visitor is.' Then without missing a beat, he continued, 'I hear you had a potential buyer come by today — Mr Crowley of the nails.' Gare let the statement hang in the air.

'Yes,' Elizabeth answered. She didn't feel like explaining to Gare how she felt at the moment about Benedict Crowley and the house. After all, if she didn't know herself how she felt, how could she explain it?

'Was he interested?' Gare questioned.

'Yes,' she said crisply, hoping he'd take the hint and drop the subject.

'Make you an offer, did he?'

'Yes, but I don't think my monetary affairs are any business of yours, Mr Stannard.'

'You are quite right, Mrs Elkins. I had no intention of asking the gory details. I was only interested to know if you had struck a deal.' He took a deep breath. 'It might interest you to know, Mrs Elkins that I am interested in not only your children but in you. You may not have noticed, but I stop by here almost every evening . . . and it's not to check on Abner's house . . . I

111

just am interested in all of you,' he went on. 'I care.'

'Please, don't say any more.' Tears were streaming down her face. She couldn't bear to hear him say any more. It was going to be hard enough to leave. He didn't have to make it any more difficult.

Josh came back downstairs. He looked at his mother and at Gare's flushed face.

'I think I'd better go,' Gare said, his voice tight.

'Where are you going, Gare?' asked Josh.

'I'm going home to take a cold shower,' he growled.

'Why?' asked the boy.

'Ask your mother,' he answered as he headed for the door. 'Although I doubt she knows.'

Nine

Early the following morning the phone rang Elizabeth awake. Sleepily, she trudged downstairs to answer it. 'Hello?'

'Good-morning, Elizabeth!' It was her mother.

'Mother, why are you calling so early? Is anything wrong?'

'No, dear. Everything's fine. Your father and I thought we'd drive up to see you and the children for the weekend . . . if that's all right with you and your schedule, that is.'

Elizabeth peered at the clock on the counter. 'That's fine. I'm not planning anything. Mother, did you know it's not even six-thirty?'

'Yes, dear. I'm sorry if I woke you. I thought maybe you'd been on the farm long enough to begin getting up with the sun . . . farmer's hours and all that.'

'We haven't got to that stage yet,' Elizabeth yawned. 'We'll be safely back in the city before we get that acclimatised.'

'Oh,' said her mother.

'Are you leaving right away?'

'Your father packed the car last night. He can't wait to get up there and try a little trout-fishing. He says you should tell the children that grandpa plans to take them fishing just like he promised. Oh, and he says to tell that nice

Gare Stannard that he'll need directions.'

'Directions? What sort of directions?'

'Directions to fishing-holes, I imagine,' answered her mother. 'I think this fishing expedition was something your father and Gare cooked up the last time we were up.'

'Oh,' said Elizabeth. 'If I see him, I'll tell him.'

'Well, your father expects you'll call him, I think. You can call him, can't you?'

'Yes, I suppose I can,' Elizabeth replied.

'You're not having another argument with that nice young man, are you, Elizabeth?'

'No, Mother,' she said stiffly. 'I'm not having another argument. I haven't run him off, if that's what you're worried about. We see a lot of him, as a matter of fact, he stops by almost every evening.'

'Good,' said her mother.

Elizabeth shook her head. 'You are impossible, Mother. Do you know that?'

'That's all right,' said her mother. 'Mothers are supposed to be.'

Elizabeth had to laugh in spite of herself. 'See you and Dad at lunchtime. Have a safe trip.'

'We will, thank you. I can't wait to see those grandchildren of mine . . . and you, too, dear. 'Bye.'

Elizabeth thought about calling Gare. Chances were he'd still be asleep. The more she thought about it, the more she liked the idea. It would serve him right to be awakened. She grinned. Plot with her parents behind her back,

114

would he. She picked up the phone and called.

'Hello?' His sleepy voice tickled her toes. She wiggled them.

'Good-morning, Mr Stannard,' she said in a bright and cheerful voice. 'This is your friendly neighbourhood wake-up service calling.'

'My what?' his groggy voice asked.

'Your friendly neighbourhood wake-up service . . .' her voice ran down. She was beginning to be less sure that this was a good idea.

'Is something wrong?' he asked.

'No, nothing is wrong. I just had a call from my parents. They asked me to call you. I'm simply being a dutiful daughter and doing what they asked.'

'That'll be the day,' he growled.

'No need to get testy, Mr Stannard.'

'Before seven on a Saturday, I'm testy.'

'Don't you want to hear the message?'

'Yes, I want to hear the message.'

'They are coming up today. Even now as we speak, they are under way. My father wants his fishing directions, which you evidently promised him.'

'Good,' said Stannard. He sounded genuinely pleased. 'I'll fix him up a map. Let's see, they should be here around noon, right?'

'Yes,' Elizabeth grumped. She had expected him to be at the very least more grouchy.

'I'll come down around noon with all the directions. I'm glad to hear they're coming. You've got nice parents.'

115

'Thank you,' Elizabeth said in a small voice.

'Is that all?'

'I guess so,' she answered.

'Am I free to climb back into my bed now, my friendly neighbourhood wake-up service lady?'

'Yes . . . go ahead.' She could think of no other sassy thing to say.

'It's nice and warm and cosy, want to join me?'

'Mr Stannard! One must not toy with the affections of wake-up service personnel!'

'Ah-ha, that's what I was afraid of,' he laughed. 'See you around noon.'

She hung up with visions of a warm, cosy Gare Stannard running through her mind. 'I need some coffee,' she said aloud. 'I'm hallucinating.'

Taking her coffee-mug in hand, Elizabeth opened the kitchen door as quietly as she could. The duck was asleep across the yard in her pen. The screen door clicked shut softly. The duck's eyes flew open and immediately she began quack-quacking to be let out.

Elizabeth had to chuckle as she went to open the pen. She wasn't a country person, that was certainly true. And she wouldn't go so far as to claim she'd learned duck in five weeks. But she could swear she knew exactly what Reina was quacking at her. 'Let me out! In the name of all that's holy in duckdom, let me out of this pen! Imagine! Keeping a fine noble duck like myself in a cage! Shame on thee, oh addle-brained featherless human!'

When Elizabeth unlatched the door to the

pen, the duck said a few phrases under her breath, then she hopped out. She followed Elizabeth back up to the house with a stream of well-chosen duck invectives delivered at full quack.

'You're a very spoiled Reina duck,' Elizabeth laughed. She went into the house to get some duck-feed. Meanwhile, the duck, to show her continuing annoyance, picked up her empty feed-plate and let it clang repeatedly on the stone steps.

With all the commotion in the yard, the children were soon up and excited to hear that their grandparents were coming. They gobbled breakfast and rushed off to gather the things they wanted to take fishing.

Gare arrived at half past eleven and almost tripped over the still-growing pile the children were collecting by the door. 'What's this?' he asked.

'We're going fishing with Grandpa,' Josh told him proudly.

'Grandpa and Grandma are coming real soon,' added Trudy, putting yet another stuffed bear on the pile.

'Are you planning to take all of this fishing?' Gare asked.

'Yep,' said Josh.

'Well,' Gare scratched his head. 'I think you've got a problem here. When you go fishing, you'll probably catch a whole lot of fish. How are you going to carry all your fish and all your toys too? Maybe you should take just one small toy that will fit in your pocket,' he suggested. 'Besides that, teddy bears aren't too fond of fishing, I understand.'

'Why not, Gare?' Trudy hugged her bears.

'I think it has something to do with not liking water. They don't like to get their fur wet. You see, teddy bear fur takes a long time to dry and sometimes it gets mouldy and turns green. Teddy bears don't like green fur.'

'Ugh!' said Trudy. 'I think you'd better stay home,' she instructed her bears.

Elizabeth was at the sink chopping celery for potato salad. 'You certainly handled that well, Mr Stannard.'

'Thank you,' he answered, coming up beside her and grabbing a handful of celery bits. She could feel the warmth of his body close to hers. He was standing so close, the reddish hairs on his arm tickled her arm when he reached for a second handful. She stopped chopping.

'What's wrong?' he asked. 'Did I take too much?'

'No.' She wanted to look up into his eyes, but didn't quite dare.

'Cassie?' He said her name so softly, it seemed to make her bones melt. The old kitchen clock ticked loudly in the silence. Very gently he tipped her chin up so that he could see her eyes. His face was soft and his eyes held hers. 'I care,' he said. 'I care a lot.'

'I know,' she answered.

Before she could say anything else, the spell was broken by car doors being shut and the children's voices calling hello out of the upstairs window.

'To be continued?' he asked with a smile.

'To be continued,' she answered.

Lunch was a jolly affair with everyone laughing and talking. The children could hardly wait to head off on their fishing expedition with their grandfather.

'This place is so lovely,' said her mother. 'I'm so glad you decided to stay the summer.'

'Me too,' Josh chimed in. 'This is the best best place we ever lived ever.'

'The really really best.' Trudy nodded her head vigorously.

'As for me,' said Gare, 'I'm glad you all decided to stay too.'

'Are you glad too, Mommy?' Josh asked.

Elizabeth blushed. 'Yes, I'm glad too,' she smiled. She might not be so glad when the time came to leave, she reflected. It was going to be difficult to leave.

'Have you had a chance to explore the rest of the state?' her father asked.

'Not really,' she answered. 'We drove into Rutland one afternoon but that's about as far as we've gotten.'

'Speaking of seeing points far afield,' Gare leaned back in his chair. 'I've been wondering if you'd like to see Mt Washington. It's only a couple of hours east of here . . . over in New Hampshire's White Mountains. It's the highest mountain in New England. You really shouldn't miss seeing it.'

'Is that the one with the railroad that runs to the summit?' asked her father.

'Yes,' Gare answered. 'It's a cog railway with a little steam locomotive . . . very picturesque. How about it, Cassie, would you like to see it?'

'Why don't you go, dear?' asked her mother.

'I don't think we'll have the time . . .' Elizabeth began.

'We could go this weekend, today,' Gare suggested.

'But my mother and father have come to visit.' Elizabeth gave him a pained look.

'They can come too,' Gare went on. 'Mt Washington shouldn't be missed. Everyone would enjoy it.'

'I know what!' her mother enthused. 'You and Gare can go. Your father and I will look after the children and the house. You can make a weekend out of it. It would do you good, Elizabeth, to get away.'

'Mother!'

'Now, Elizabeth, don't be an old fuddy-duddy, dear. Take it from your mother, people go away together for weekends all the time these days.'

'I know that, Mother . . . I was just thinking that the children will probably feel left out . . . and you and Dad, too, for that matter.'

'I want to go fishing with Grandpa,' said Josh. 'I've been looking forward to fishing all day.'

'Me too,' Trudy agreed. 'I've been looking forward to fishing all my life!'

'And I want to go fishing with Josh and Trudy,' said her father. He winked at her. 'I've been waiting for this for over sixty years.'

'I'm being railroaded!' Elizabeth said with exasperation. 'Did you all plan this ahead of time?' She eyed the three adults suspiciously.

'Cross my heart,' grinned Gare. 'We did not plan anything ahead of time.'

'You're just too suspicious,' said her mother.

In the end she decided to go. Not because she had been pushed into it, but because she felt like taking a break. It would be fun to see some of the countryside. Heaven only knew when she might get back up this way again. And then, she did like Stannard . . . not as a boyfriend or a lover . . . even though that might be very nice . . . but as a good friend and neighbour.

The weather was superb, sunny and warm with a nice cooling breeze. They were heading east into New Hampshire and had just crossed the Connecticut River. 'Tell me truthfully,' Elizabeth began, 'did you and my parents set this up?'

'No, we didn't,' he grinned. 'Great minds run the same track, as the saying goes.'

'More like — birds of a feather flock together — if you ask me,' she replied. 'You're a bunch of mischief-makers, the whole lot of you. I shouldn't allow you in the same room together — maybe not even in the same state.'

He laughed. 'You certainly are one suspicious lady.'

'I have reason to be,' she answered. 'And just for your information, Mr Stannard, I did not come away on this little jaunt with you to climb into bed with you. We can share a room if need be, but we will not share a bed.' For some reason her cheeks flamed red.

'Whatever you say . . . though I don't recall requesting a shared bed, did I?' He glanced over at her.

'No,' she answered, 'you didn't. But I just want to set things straight at the beginning — no false pretences — no expectations.'

'I've no expectations,' he answered. 'I only want to enjoy seeing Mt Washington again and hope you enjoy sharing the experience with me.'

'Good, then we agree,' she replied. She sighed. Why was it, she wondered, that life was so complicated. It seemed one practically needed a written, notarized contract for a simple date.

The sky over Mt Washington was almost completely clear. Every so often a puffy white cloud would bump into the summit and obscure the top from view.

'That's quite a mountain,' Elizabeth remarked.

'Wait until you get to the top,' Gare replied.

They could see the tracks of the cog railroad, a silver ribbon on the mountain's side. Clouds of steam and smoke told of the little train's progress up the silver rail.

'The steepest inclined railroad in the world' read a roadside sign.

Gare turned off onto a side road that led through stands of tall pines to the base of the mountain. They parked the car and Gare went to get tickets. He came back holding the two tickets. 'We just got lucky. I didn't know we needed reservations. There had just been a cancellation for the next trip to the top. Talk about luck.' He shook his head. 'Come along, lady fair, we are just about to depart to one of the far ends of the earth.'

He took her hand and they boarded a gaily-painted, old-fashioned wooden railway coach.

Almost at once a little chugging engine came up behind the line of coaches. In a great burst of steam it blew its whistle.

'What a strange looking engine,' Elizabeth remarked. 'It looks like something out of a Walt Disney movie. Why did they build it on a slant?'

'Boilers work best on the level,' Gare explained. 'These little engines spend most of their time on an incline. By tipping the boiler forward, it stays relatively flat on its trip up the mountain.'

With an 'All Aboard' from the conductor and another blast of its whistle, the little train began its ascent.

They passed through tall pines, the little train clanking up the track, the rolling cogs underneath catching on the ratchet that ran between the rails.

'This train works something like a clock,' Gare explained. 'A clock has cogs that turn together to run the hands. This railroad has cogs that turn to catch the ratchet, pulling the train up the mountain.'

Halfway up the mountain the train stopped. The trainmen, who were all young men in overalls and bright bandanas, climbed off and manually turned the switch onto a siding. The train then pulled onto the siding and waited for the train coming down the mountain to pass by on the main track. After the passing, with everyone in both trains waving back and forth, the switching process was repeated and the train continued on up the mountain.

As they climbed slowly up the mountain, the trees thinned out, then disappeared altogether. Hikers waved to the passengers as the train chugged by. Elizabeth waved and waved just like everyone else.

The weather was glorious and the view, as they climbed ever higher, was spectacular.

Elizabeth turned to Gare and smiled. 'I'm really glad I came. This is wonderful.'

'I'm really glad you came too,' he smiled in

return. 'This is one of my favourite sights in all of New England.'

Near the top of mountain, everything was shrouded in clouds. The miles and miles of view suddenly disappeared.

'It's spooky,' Elizabeth laughed. 'It feels like a strange and alien land.'

'Yes,' Gare agreed. 'It is.'

The clouds swirled and the concrete summit-building came into view — then disappeared as quickly.

'Not a very handsome building,' Elizabeth remarked. 'I was expecting something with more charm.'

'I don't think charm was uppermost on the list when they designed something that had to live up here. They were just hoping to come up with something that wouldn't blow away.'

The little train wheezed to a stop. The passengers all climbed out on the barren rock ground. The wind was so strong they all had to lean at an angle to walk against it. Elizabeth wrapped her thin, flapping sweater around her chilled body. Gare put a protective arm around her. 'I'm beginning to see what you meant about blowing away.' The wind whipped the words from her mouth.

Just as quickly as the cloud had come, it blew on over the mountain. The miles and miles of clear view of mountains and valleys appeared, bathed in bright sunlight. It happened so instantaneously, and was so dramatic, that a chorus of

'Ahhhs' arose from the passengers.

Almost everyone went inside the summit building, except a few hardy souls who had brought winter-weight jackets and woollen hats.

'I can't believe it's so cold up here.' Elizabeth shivered even after they were inside the warm building.

'This mountain has the most severe weather in New England,' Gare explained. 'The highest wind ever recorded on the face of the earth was recorded here — 231 mph.'

'231 miles per hour!' Elizabeth gasped. 'No wonder this place looks like a bomb shelter!'

After touring the small weather museum, there was just time enough to buy some postcards before the departure of the train was announced. The passengers laughingly braved the fierce wind to reboard the train.

As the little train came down from the summit, another cloud rolled in to the mountain top. It was a small cloud. They could see it flit and surge as the wind tried to get it over the top.

'I feel as though I've had a front-row seat on creation,' Elizabeth said. 'It's a great privilege!'

'This is my fifth trip to the top and I still feel that way,' Gare agreed. 'It is, indeed, awesome!'

'I really do want to thank you again for getting me here — by hook or by crook, or however you did it,' Elizabeth chuckled. 'It's unforgettable.'

'You're welcome, my pleasure.'

They watched the mountain scenery roll by the windows.

'I can't tell you how relaxing this is. I had forgotten how much fun field-trips are.'

'That comes from too much living in the future,' Gare said matter-of-factly.

'Too much living in the future?' Elizabeth questioned. 'What do you mean by that?'

'It's very easy to slip into,' Gare went on. 'We all do it. It's when we forget to smell the flowers under our feet, forget that today is a gift too. When all our thoughts and work are focused on a day — or days — in tomorrow, it's so easy to get enmeshed in future thinking and overlook the only day we can count on as a sure thing — today!'

'You're right,' Elizabeth nodded. 'I know I'm very guilty of that. It's hard not to be.'

'I know,' Gare answered. 'I do it too.'

'Maybe I can reform a bit,' she grinned, 'with a little help from my friends, my parents and one kind neighbour.'

'I'm at your service,' he answered. 'Tell you what, you remind me to appreciate today and I'll remind you. Is that a deal?'

'Yes, it's a deal,' she agreed.

By the time the little train reached the valley floor, it was late afternoon. 'I think we'd better start looking for a room.' Gare watched her face to gauge her reaction.

'Fine,' she said, her face giving away nothing.

They tried the grand old sprawling hotel that stood red-roofed and proud at the base of the mountain. There were no rooms available.

'Sorry, sir,' said the desk clerk, 'we're booked weeks in advance this time of the year.'

'Too bad,' Elizabeth said sadly. 'But I can certainly see why. This place is like walking into a time warp. I feel as though we've stepped into 1891!'

The desk clerk smiled. 'That's the feeling we intend to evoke. Nice, isn't it?'

'Yes, lovely,' Elizabeth nodded.

'Maybe next time,' Gare added.

As they left the hotel, Elizabeth gave him a sideways glance. 'What's this about "next time" That's tomorrow thinking — remember today!'

'Right!' he replied. 'Onward and upward with today!'

They finally found a room in a rather run-down boarding-house in a small town twenty miles from the mountain. The literature they picked up from the landlady said the town was famous as one of the only pollen-free places in the world. People came from everywhere, it said, to live here without sneezing and itchy red eyes.

Elizabeth looked at the room and frowned. A bare bulb hung from the ceiling, the one bed squeaked and complained at the merest touch. But it all appeared to be clean, if painfully plain.

'Do you want to look further?' Gare whispered the question so the landlady couldn't hear.

Elizabeth raised her eyebrows. 'We better be content with this, I guess,' she whispered back. She had lost count of the number of motels with no-vacancy signs. This was probably the only unoccupied bed in New Hampshire tonight.

The landlady handed them a stack of towels and left.

Elizabeth pointed to the bed. 'I'll take the right, you take the left — and it's no-man's-land down the middle — agreed?'

'Whatever suits your fancy,' he answered.

They had a wonderful home-cooked meal at an unpretentious house turned restaurant down the block.

It was called 'Ma McCormick's' and everything was served home-style from fresh-baked bread to cherry-pie.

Afterwards, they strolled slowly back towards the boarding-house.

'Could we walk around a bit?' Elizabeth asked. 'I feel like someone should roll me down the street. I ate too much.'

'I know exactly how you feel,' Gare agreed. 'A walk is an excellent idea.'

The night air was clear and cool. They strolled to the green in the centre of town where local musicians were setting up for a concert in the bandstand.

They walked slowly around the green listening to the sprightly marches of John Philip Sousa and then the romantic tunes of Rogers and Hammerstein. She tripped and he caught her hand to keep her from falling — and then didn't let go.

The feel of her hand in his felt good to Elizabeth very good in fact. She was, she told herself, enjoying today — smelling the flowers of now. All she had to do was keep her head and all would be fine.

Ten

After the concert they turned towards the boarding-house and the one iron bed.

Elizabeth undressed in the bathroom. She put on her gown and her robe and wrapped the belt securely.

While Gare was in the bathroom, she rolled a bolster-roll from the bedspread and laid it down the middle line of the bed. When Gare came out, she pointed to the makeshift demarcation line. 'I made a divider,' she said.

'Oh?' He raised his eyebrows.

'That will just make it easier for each of us to know where we belong,' she said reasonably. He didn't comment.

They turned off the light and climbed into bed, each on a side. The old bed groaned and creaked.

She had thought she'd fall immediately to sleep; instead she lay there, hardly daring to move because of the noise it would make. She watched the breeze sweep the curtain back and forth at the window.

People passed by in the street below, their voices fading in and out. She thought of being someone else, somewhere else — in another time, in another life. She thought of her dream of being married to Stannard and having sixteen kids. She grinned to herself. A far-off clock rang midnight.

'Twelve,' she said in a whisper, not even realizing until she had said it, that she was speaking out loud.

'What's that?' Stannard asked.

'I'm sorry,' she said. 'I was counting the bells. I'm sorry I woke you up.'

'I wasn't asleep,' he answered.

'You either? How long have we been lying here?'

'An hour maybe,' he answered.

'We probably ate too much,' she suggested.

They both were silent for a while.

Elizabeth thought again of the sixteen children and began chuckling quietly to herself. She covered her mouth to keep from making any noise, but she couldn't help jiggling ever so slightly. The old bed detected her movement and began sighing softly in its springs.

'What are you doing?' Gare asked.

'Oh my,' gasped Elizabeth, seeing at once the humour in the whole situation, 'I'm laughing.'

'I thought so,' he answered. 'Why not share the joke with your bedfellow?'

So she told her dream.

'Sixteen children and number seventeen in the planning stages!' he laughed. 'You know, don't you, that your dream reveals your sexual need for me?'

'Maybe it reveals the absurdity of the whole situation,' she countered. 'Sure, it might be fun to hop into bed with you . . .'

'In case you haven't noticed,' he interrupted,

'you have . . . is this fun?'

'Well, no . . . oh you know what I mean. You didn't let me finish.'

'Go ahead, finish.'

'What I was going to say is that grown-up, mature people know that instant gratification is not the way to go. Life is enriched by long-term, on-going commitments, not by one-night stands.'

'You also agreed with me today that we must learn better how to live in the now, in today. We didn't meet yesterday either, by the way.'

'I know, I know,' she answered. 'I would like to go to bed with you. I admit it. But I don't think I should. I don't want to turn my life around for you. I don't want to need you.'

'I didn't ask you to turn your life around for me,' he answered carefully. 'You don't have to need me. I can't make you need me . . . nor would I if I could. Your need must come from you. I'm not ever going to try to twist your arm. But I will tell you . . . I need *you*.'

She lay there for a very long time, saying nothing. Tears leaked out of the corners of her eyes and ran down into her ears. She sniffed and wiped her eyes.

'Are you crying?' he asked. 'Don't cry over me.'

'I'll cry if I want!' she answered. 'And for your information, I'm not crying over you!'

'Then why are you crying?'

'I'm crying because I want you too,' she blubbered.

'Are you sure?'

'Yes, I'm sure!' she answered with some heat.

'Because I sure don't want to make love to someone who feels sorry for me,' he continued.

'I don't feel sorry for you!' she replied hotly.

'Then, why do you want to make love to me?'

'Because I care about you!' she shouted at him.

There was a banging on the wall. 'Quiet down in there! Whatever you're going to do, do it quietly!'

They both sat up in bed and burst into quiet gales of laughter. They rocked back and forth with their hands over their mouths.

When the laughter had wound down, Gare took the bedspread roll out of the bed. 'We don't need this, do we?'

She shook her head no.

So gently did he touch her skin and kiss her mouth, she could barely stand it. Now that she had given him permission, she wanted to roar right into it. But he took her step by step ever deeper into the world of passion. The slow progression made her need for him burn brighter and hotter. She thought he would never get around to taking off her nightgown. When he did, she sighed at the exquisite pleasure it gave to feel the silken material glide slowly up her torso and over her head.

She lunged at his lips and he gently pulled back. 'Not so fast, my love. Slowly, slowly . . . savour it, my sweet.'

He ran his fingertips lightly up her legs, up her

sides and down her arms. Never before had she felt such tickling soft fingerings on her skin. Her body shivered, one quake following the next, building crescendo on crashing, rolling crescendo.

When at last they reached the summit, Elizabeth felt her body melt away into the most delicious floating mist.

Slowly she came back to earth. Slowly she poured herself back into her body. What had happened, she wondered? She had been a married woman. She had made love countless times. She had two children, for heaven's sake. What was going on here? Why was this so much better than she remembered? Now Elizabeth, she told herself, it's been a long time. That's probably reason enough.

'Comfortable?' Gare asked, cradling her curled-up body in his.

'Ummm, yes,' she answered.

Of course that was it. It was just a nice drink of fresh water to someone who had been too long thirsty.

The next morning she awoke to see a fully-dressed Gare coming in the door with two mugs of coffee and a small white paper bag with the name of a bakery scrolled on its side. 'Good-morning,' he smiled brightly. 'I hope you slept well. I know I did.' His eyes twinkled.

She sat up and rubbed her eyes.

'You must have slept well,' he grinned, 'you look devastatingly beautiful.'

She looked down and saw that she had nothing on. She blushed and covered herself.

'You even blush in a most becoming colour.' He put down the coffee and opened the crisp white bag. 'Apple Danish.' He held the open bag under her nose. 'The baker said they were the most popular roll in the shop. I took his word for it. Shall we give them our most critical taste test?'

She couldn't help but smile at his ebullient good humour. And to tell the truth, she did feel much refreshed. It was probably that special breed of pollen free air the town was said to possess.

The Danish were excellent, as was the coffee.

Not that she would have wanted it any other way, but she wondered why he had got up and not awakened her. Why had he dressed and gone out? She would have expected him to want more sex. Wasn't that the way things usually worked? Was once enough? Was she simply a conquest completed? Would it be on to the next one now? What was it Tommy had said of Gare? 'He can pick a winner every time,' that was it. Didn't that signify a whole line of women, of which she might be the latest?

'A penny for your thoughts,' he smiled.

'I guess I'd better get dressed,' she smiled back. 'That seems to be the order of the day.'

'Oh?' He stopped in mid-sip of his coffee. 'Did you have other things in mind, my good lady?'

'No-no-no,' she answered in what she hoped

looked and sounded like a light-hearted manner. She laughed lightly. 'I was just making conversation, that's all. Last night was fun but we mustn't make a habit of it. That would be dangerous, don't you agree?'

'Hmmm . . . maybe . . . I suppose so,' he muttered through his apple Danish.

'Can't play with dynamite without getting blown up sooner or later,' she added.

He raised his eyebrows but didn't say anything.

She was anxious to get dressed. The more she talked about last night, the more her body wanted — demanded — more. Dynamite was the right word for it. And dangerous was the correct adjective. She wished he'd leave so she could get out of bed and into her clothes without feeling embarrassed . . . and without making a detour to throw her naked body against his, which is what she felt like doing.

As though he had read her mind, he said — 'This coffee tastes like another cup. How about you? Would you like a refill?'

'Yes, please.'

'Back in a flash,' he grinned and left the room.

She dressed in a hurry. She had to rebutton her blouse twice. For some silly reason she was very nervous. When Gare returned, she was ready. They sipped their coffee and went to check out.

The day was overcast and somewhat chilly. The tops of the mountains in the distance were shrouded in clouds.

'We certainly were lucky yesterday,' Elizabeth scanned the sky. It was grey from horizon to horizon.

'Yes, we were,' Gare agreed . . . 'and weatherwise too.' He looked at her to see if she had caught his meaning.

She looked up at him, smiled ruefully and shook her head.

Halfway home they passed through a town bustling with tourists and traffic. 'Popular place,' Elizabeth commented. 'That fellow Josh tried to do in with the nails comes from here.'

'The potential buyer?' Gare questioned. 'He comes from here? Funny he would want a farmhouse in Vermont.'

'Maybe he doesn't like all the hustle and bustle. Maybe he wants to get away to a little peace and quiet.'

'Maybe,' he answered thoughtfully. 'You feel like some breakfast?'

'That sounds like a good idea to me,' she replied.

They passed a diner with a parking-lot full of cars. 'Looks like they might have good food in here. Shall we try it?'

'Suits me,' she answered.

They ordered ham and eggs and orange-juice from a talkative waitress. 'Busy place you've got here,' Gare commented.

'We've got the best food in town,' she answered. 'Lots of fancy restaurants coming in here that charge all sorts of outlandish prices, but we're still as busy as ever. Can't beat good food at fair prices, I always say.'

'You happen to know Benedict Crowley?' Elizabeth asked.

'Of course,' she nodded her head vigorously. 'Everyone knows him. He's the biggest developer in town. That mall across the street, that's his. And he's got two condos — one's all rented called the Silver Swan. The other one's not even finished yet and I hear he's got it almost full. He calls it Blackbird Meadows. Guess he's partial to birds. You folks looking to buy a place around here? Those condos are real nice but you need a pocketful of money to get close to them.'

'No, we're from Vermont,' Gare answered.

'Oh well . . . always nice to have Vermonters over for a visit, I always say.' She slipped her orderbook in her apron and gave the table a quick wipe.

When the waitress had left, Elizabeth hissed — 'A developer! Benedict Crowley is a developer! He said he'd keep Uncle Abner's just as it is and not change a thing!'

Gare frowned. 'Of course we don't know for sure what he's planning . . .'

Elizabeth sighed. 'That's true, but he didn't act quite right. Now that I think about it, he didn't act right at all. He was in too much of a hurry. He hardly looked.'

'I'm not trying to start an argument,' Gare said carefully, 'but do you really care what happens to Uncle Abner's?'

'Yes, I do,' Elizabeth answered rather hotly.

'Well, I just wondered,' Gare went on. 'You do still want to sell it, don't you?'

'Yes, I want to sell it,' she replied. 'But that doesn't mean I want someone to spoil it. It's a fine old place. I don't want it changed. I told the real-estate broker that was a condition of the sale. I'm not totally heartless, you know.'

'No, I didn't think that you were,' he answered.

All the way home they spoke together only of safe subjects. They didn't mention Uncle Abner's, or Benedict Crowley, or the momentous thing that had happened between them last night.

When Elizabeth climbed into her own bed in Uncle Abner's that night, she felt the old house settle down around her. Yes, she really did care what happened to this house. It felt good. It felt like home. It would be akin to murder to let someone destroy what it was and how it was. It was too bad she couldn't stay here herself to defend it. She couldn't afford to keep it. She had to let it go. It was too bad there weren't better laws regulating what developers like Benedict Crowley could do with places like Uncle Abner's. They shouldn't be allowed to come in and tear down places that touched the heart.

The more she thought about it, the more upset she became. 'I should fight this,' she said aloud. Then she lay back and heard what she had just said . . . 'I should fight this.'

'Maybe,' she said slowly, 'just maybe, I should reconsider some things.' She shivered. Her body was remembering last night. 'Maybe . . .' she whispered as she fell asleep . . . 'I should reconsider a lot of things.'

Eleven

She awoke the following morning with the taste of adventure in her mouth. She hadn't known how sweet it could be to have a new direction to ponder. She reminded herself that she didn't have to change her mind. Until she had thought it through completely to her satisfaction, she would tell nobody. It wouldn't be fair to get anyone's hopes up prematurely. 'Don't celebrate yet,' she spoke aloud to the corner of the room where she had decided Uncle Abner's ghost hovered. 'I may not change one thing. I'm only taking some other options under consideration.'

At breakfast Josh and Trudy were full of tales of fishing. They had caught twelve rainbow trout between them. Grandma, they said, had cooked some of them last night and they were 'soooo good' to quote Trudy. 'Why don't you cook trout, Mommy?' Trudy asked.

'I don't know how to skin a fish and cook it,' Elizabeth replied.

'Tsk, tsk, tsk,' said her mother. 'It's simple. You don't "skin" a trout. You don't scale them either. Simply clean them, drip them in a batter and fry. You can even fry them without a coating. It's very easy.'

'Since when do you know how to cook a fresh-caught trout?' Elizabeth asked her mother. 'I don't remember ever seeing you do that.'

'Mothers have lives before their children are born,' her mother replied. 'Remember I mentioned that cabin in the Michigan woods?' Her mother looked thoughtful. 'We never went camping again after you were born. I'm not sure why. Too much trouble with a baby, I guess, and no place we knew of close by. Too bad. You might have grown up feeling differently about this place,' she added somewhat wistfully.

'I think this is a nice place, a fine place, no matter what any of you think I think,' Elizabeth replied with heat. She almost said she was reconsidering her decision to sell, but bit her tongue.

'I didn't mean to ruffle your feathers, dear,' her mother responded. 'I'm sorry. I was only speaking for myself. If your father and I were twenty years younger, we'd buy this place from you. We're that taken with it. But,' she hurried on to explain, 'we fully realize that you must do what you think is best. And we will stand a hundred per cent behind whatever decision you make.'

'Thank you, Mother. I appreciate that very much. It's hard having to make unpopular decisions.'

'I know, dear. Did you and Gare have a good weekend?'

'Yes, we did. Mt Washington is truly an awesome sight and then some.'

'That's nice, dear.'

Elizabeth could see her mother trying to formulate a question about her relationship with Stannard. She wanted to know if it had heated

143

up any, but she was having trouble finding suitable words.

'Gare and I had a great time. If you want to know any more, you'll have to ask him,' she grinned.

'Don't think I won't,' answered her mother.

'I was afraid of that,' Elizabeth laughed.

'But unfortunately, your father and I have to leave right after lunch. I have a dentist appointment first thing in the morning. Drat!' she grinned. 'Oh I almost forgot, your father and I want to take the children out for an hour or so more of fishing, if that's all right with you.'

'That's fine,' Elizabeth answered. 'That will give me time to run into town for some groceries. We're almost out of duck-food.'

'Reina would probably bomb the house if she knew that,' laughed her mother.

'That's right,' Elizabeth agreed. 'Lucky us, we've got the only subversive duck in Vermont.'

When she got back with the groceries, there was nobody home but the raccoon. 'Oh no,' she sighed. 'The neighbourhood nuisance has broken out again.' The fat, half-grown raccoon came burrring out to meet her.

She tried to take the groceries in the house, but the raccoon wouldn't leave them alone. He was either in the bags in the car or following her into the kitchen to see what was on the counter.

'Okay, smart one,' she looked at him in exasperation. She threw him a couple of cookies.

'Eat these and leave my groceries alone.' The cookies kept him occupied for a few minutes, but before she could make another trip, he was at the bags again. She picked him up and put him on her shoulders. He burred at her. 'Let's see if I can outsmart you, Mr Smarty-pants.' She knew he was afraid to jump to the ground. He could walk down her body to the ground, but only if she stood still. Much to her surprise, her idea worked. As long as she kept moving, the coon was stuck on her shoulders. She moved quickly to bring in all the bags from the car. Then she took a handful of cookies outside, put the coon down and went inside and latched the screen door.

She stood in the doorway and grinned at the fat coon gobbling the cookies. 'You know, Coonish, it was a pleasure to finally outsmart you. I think I deserve a medal of some sort.'

She had almost all of the groceries put away before the coon came burring his indignation at the locked door. 'When are you going to leave home, old boy?' she asked.

'Burrr . . . churr,' said the coon.

'When are your sex glands going to kick in? Isn't it about time you checked out the girls?' Gare had told her the coon would eventually hear the call of the wild and leave for the life of a wild raccoon.

When the children and her parents returned from fishing, the children were delighted to see the coon had escaped again and had come to pay them a visit.

'He's sure awful smart,' said Josh.

'He likes us,' said Trudy.

'He likes our cookies.' Elizabeth shook her head.

After lunch her parents left. Josh went upstairs to read. Elizabeth settled down with the Vermont Law School catalogue to try to come to some decision. And Trudy went outside to play with the raccoon.

An hour or more went by before Josh came back downstairs to get a glass of milk.

'What are you reading, Mommy?' He sat down beside her at the table with his glass of milk.

'A catalogue,' she answered.

'About what?' he asked.

'It's about the Vermont Law School,' she replied.

He took a gulp of milk. She saw his eyes grow larger as a thought occurred to him. 'Does that mean you might go to school there?' He almost upset his glass.

'I don't know,' Elizabeth answered.

'Does that mean we might stay here?' He took the thought easily to its logical conclusion.

'I don't know, Josh.'

'But maybe it does?' he persisted.

'Maybe,' she answered.

'Oh boy!' His eyes were alight with excitement. He got up and dashed across the room.

'Joshua!' she called after him. 'Don't get so excited over a maybe. It's only a *maybe*,' she stressed the word.

'I know, I know.' He flew out of the door.

In a minute or two the door whoosed open again. In came Josh, and Trudy with the raccoon in her arms. Her little face was all smiles.

Elizabeth cleared her throat. 'Now Joshua, I told you it was only a maybe. Maybes are not yeses. Maybe means perhaps yes or perhaps no.'

'Coonish wants us to stay, don't you, Coonish?' Trudy waved the coon's paw at Elizabeth.

'I know,' said her mother. 'But we can't make decisions about our lives based on the whim of a raccoon.' Or children either, she was thinking.

At the sound of tyres on gravel, the children ran to the door. 'It's Gare! It's Gare!' they both whooped and were out of the door before Elizabeth had time to caution them.

Gare came through the door a moment later. 'What's this, I hear?' His eyes, too, were alight with excitement.

'I feel as though I'm speaking a foreign language around here,' Elizabeth began. 'Nobody seems to understand that there's a perfectly good word — MAYBE — in the English language. I said MAYBE we're staying. I am considering it — that's all. Only considering.'

'I see,' said Gare, the light in his eyes dimming some. 'Why don't you troops find something else to do?' he suggested to the children, 'so your mom and I can talk adult talk.'

'I'm reading a good book,' said Josh. 'I'll go upstairs.'

'Coonish and I will go outside,' Trudy offered.

'Good,' said Gare. 'Thank you for your co-operation. I appreciate that.'

When the children were out of earshot, Gare smiled. 'I can't pretend I'm not pleased to hear you're considering staying in Vermont.'

'Everyone . . . you . . . my parents . . . the children . . . all make it awfully hard for me to make an unemotional decision. It's important to make an unemotional decision, unemotional choices.'

'I suppose,' Gare responded, 'it depends on what you're making a decision about. It seems to me some choices are best made emotionally.'

'Such as?'

'Well, since you asked, decisions of the heart. Wouldn't emotion be involved in those?'

'Of course emotions are involved in those, but it's still best to divorce your emotions from your decisions as much as possible.'

'Take last night for instance,' he pressed his point. 'Did you divorce your emotions from your decision to make love with me?'

'In a way,' she answered.

'In a way?' His eyebrows shot up. 'In a way . . . I'm not made of stone, you know. Maybe city men are. I've been very patient with you.'

'Patient with me?' she stormed. 'Who asked you to be patient with me? Certainly I never did!

That's all your idea!'

'You're probably right,' he agreed. 'Maybe you should go back to the city. Maybe that's where you really do belong. Maybe I've been wrong all along to hope you'd change your heart and mind. You yourself reminded me once of what I said about my great-grandmother Stannard . . . that she knew what she wanted. Maybe it's sheer folly to get in the way of what a strong-minded woman wants. I'm truly sorry . . . sorry for both of us . . . Elizabeth.' With that, he turned and went out of the door, closing it softly behind him.

Elizabeth heard the sound of wheels on gravel as he backed out of the drive. She couldn't bear to turn around and watch the blue pick-up disappear from view. She sat at the table, tears streaming down her face. How had she managed to make such a mess of things? Just when everything seemed on the verge of taking new directions, all the pieces came apart.

After a long while, she managed to pull herself together enough to begin something for the children's supper. She didn't feel like eating. She felt more like throwing up.

She called Josh down to eat and then went to the door to call Trudy. The little girl didn't answer. Elizabeth went outside to call her. She walked around the house. Trudy was nowhere to be seen. She checked the barn. She called. No Trudy.

Josh came outside to see what the problem

was. 'Where's Trudy, Mom?'

'Josh,' she tried to sound calm, 'I can't find her!'

'Don't worry, Mommy. She's probably down in the meadow. I'll go get her.' He ran down the meadow path with Elizabeth following, her heart in her throat.

Before they got down the ravine, they could easily see that Trudy wasn't there. 'Sqwack, quack,' said Reina duck, arriving a few minutes behind and flapping her wings in agitation.

They called and called, the duck squawked. There was no answer from Trudy.

Elizabeth ran back to the house. 'I'm going to call Gare,' she told Josh. 'You stay out here and keep calling. Maybe she'll answer. But stay right here. I don't need two lost children.' She looked at the woods that started at the edge of the meadow. The deep, dark, wild woods. She longed for sidewalks and buildings. She should have stayed where she belonged, where children didn't get lost because you never let them out of your sight.

The phone rang five times before Stannard answered. 'Hello.' He sounded angry.

'Gare, this is Elizabeth. Trudy's lost!'

'I'll be right there!'

It seemed an eternity before the blue pick-up sped into the yard.

Elizabeth ran up to him. 'We've checked everywhere. She's not here! Oh Gare, where's my baby?' She burst into tears.

He gathered her in his arms. 'There, there. She can't have got too far. Don't worry. We'll find her.'

The minutes dragged by. Dusk was coming on. Gare came back to the house after a quick search of the woods behind the house. 'I'm going to call for help.'

'Oh my God!' Elizabeth cried. 'What's happened to her, Gare? What's happened to my baby?'

'Try to calm down,' he said softly. 'She's got to be out there somewhere. It's just a matter of adding some extra eyes before we lose the light altogether. Don't worry. We will find her.'

He called the local fire department and then some fellow wardens. In a short while the yard filled up with cars and tight-lipped men and several women.

Gare directed the search, sending groups in different directions. 'Which way should I go?' Elizabeth asked.

'No,' Gare ordered. 'You and Josh stay here. Someone has to stay here.'

'But I want to come too.'

'I know,' Gare put his arm around her. 'I know you do. It's hard to stay behind, but you're the most logical one to stay here. She might show up on her own and finding the house empty, get scared and leave again. Do you understand?'

She nodded, tears streaming silently down her face.

Time passed. Elizabeth paced. Josh sat in a

corner, his knees pulled up under his chin, watching her. 'Don't be worried, Mommy. Gare will find Trudy.'

'Yes, yes, of course, she answered, not wanting to alarm the boy any further.

'Trudy likes the woods,' Josh went on. 'She's not afraid of the woods . . . even in the dark. She's brave.'

'Oh?' answered Elizabeth.

'No, really, Mommy. She's not afraid. I asked her once and she said so.'

Elizabeth didn't answer, she simply shook her head.

'Gare told us that woods are just like our yard,' the boy went on, 'except there's more trees. And he said the dark is the same outside as it is inside. He said if we aren't afraid of our room in the dark, we shouldn't be afraid in the dark outside either.'

Elizabeth had stopped pacing and was listening to her son. 'Do you really think Trudy thinks that?'

'Yes, Mom,' he answered solemnly.

Elizabeth sat down. 'I hope you're right, Joshua. I hate to think of her out there and being scared to death.'

'Like you, huh, Mom?'

Elizabeth had to smile slightly. 'Yes,' she nodded, 'like me.'

Time limped along. Elizabeth looked at the clock and then looked again two minutes later expecting to see an hour at least had passed. It seemed to her that she and Josh were caught in a time warp somewhere, disconnected from the rest of the world where time progressed and things were sensible and sane, and little girls didn't get lost in the woods. Please, dear God, she prayed. Let her be safe. Let her be found.

Sudden sounds of laughter made her start. 'Mom, they've found her!' Josh was up in an instant and flying out of the door.

Elizabeth ran too, her tears beginning again.

Coming into the circle of light in the yard was the search-party. Gare was carrying Trudy. He put her down and the little girl ran into her mother's arms. 'Mommy, Mommy,' she cried. She pulled back and looked at her mother's tear-streaked face. 'Mommy, why are you crying?'

'Because you were lost,' Josh explained.

'No, I wasn't lost,' said the little girl. 'I was in the woods. Home was lost.'

The searchers, gathered around the little family, all laughed.

'Coonish and I went for a walk,' Trudy explained in her careful four-year-old way. 'Then we took a nap inside a big tree just like Winnie the Pooh! When I woke up, Coonish was gone and it was so dark I didn't know where home was.'

'She was inside a hollow tree,' Gare explained. 'That's why we didn't find her right away.'

'See, Mom, I told you she was fine,' Josh interjected. 'Were you scared, Trudy?' he asked his sister.

'No,' said the little girl. 'I 'membered what Gare told us about being scared of the dark, so I wasn't.'

Elizabeth hugged her daughter and invited the searchers in for coffee. They were friendly people, people she had seen around town. She could have hugged them all, she was so grateful for their help.

One of them was Tommy of Tommy's Garage. 'Not a very good introduction to our good state,' he said to her. 'I hope you don't hold it against us . . . Elizabeth, isn't it?'

'Yes, it is Elizabeth,' she answered. 'But Gare calls me Cassie . . . you can call me Cassie.' She refilled his mug. 'And as far as an introduction to Vermont goes, I think it's wonderful. I can't tell you how good you all make me feel coming to help us like this. I can't thank you enough.'

'It's the way things are up here,' Tommy smiled. 'We help out. Sooner or later everyone needs a helping hand. We're glad to do it.'

When the children had been put to bed and all the searchers but one had left, Elizabeth sat over her coffee-cup, staring into its depths. Gare sat across from her. 'Can you see your future in there?' he asked.

'I think it's tea-leaves you read fortunes with, but yes,' she smiled, 'I think I can.'

'Would you care to share it?'

'I see a deep, dark wood,' she intoned. 'And I see a woman coming out of it. It looks like . . . no . . . yes, it's myself! I'm carrying something. Wait

a minute . . . it's . . . it's . . . for heaven's sake . . .
it's Coonish!'

He chuckled. 'Is that all?'

She looked up at him. 'Where is Coonish by
the way? He hasn't come back here.'

'The call of the wild, no doubt.' Gare grinned.
'He's probably having himself a high old time
out in them thar woods.'

'That goes on a lot up here in the woods,
doesn't it?'

'Sure,' he answered. 'It's supposed to. That's
the way Mother Nature intended it to be.'

'And wouldn't you say it's folly to go against
Mother Nature?'

'Most usually,' he answered.

'Wait a minute!' Elizabeth was peering into
her coffee-cup again. 'I see something else in
here. Someone else is coming out of those
woods. It's you!'

'Me?'

'Yes, it's definitely you. You've got something
in your hands too and you're handing it to me. I
can't quite see what it is . . .'

'What is it?' He got up and came around to
stand beside her.

'Can you see it?' she asked.

He peered into the black coffee. 'Could it be a
diploma?'

'Maybe,' she answered. 'Yes, yes it is! It's a diploma from the Vermont Law School. How
about that!'

'How about that!' he replied.

'Look at that!' Elizabeth exclaimed.

'What do you see now?' he asked softly.

'You're kissing me! How about that! Can you see that?'

'Like this?' he asked and took her in his arms.

Twelve

There was great celebrating around Uncle Abner's house the next morning when Elizabeth . . . alias Cassie . . . told the children that they would be staying in Vermont.

'Are we marrying Gare too?' Josh asked.

'Yes, let's do that too, Mommy, can we?' asked Trudy.

'All in good time,' Elizabeth grinned at her children. 'All in good time.'

They were in the middle of breakfast when Benedict Crowley came to the door. 'Good-morning, Mrs Elkins. Fine day. And I do believe it's about to get even finer for you.'

'Good-morning, Mr Crowley.' She returned his greeting but left him standing on the stoop. 'Before you go any further, I think I should tell you I've changed my mind about selling.'

'Bad move, Mrs Elkins, bad move.' Mr Crowley looked thunderous.

Josh came over and stood beside his mother. He crossed his arms and frowned at Mr Crowley.

'I don't know if you know anything about the law, Mrs Elkins, but I can sue you for withdrawing your property. Tsk, tsk. And here I came prepared to make you an even better offer, Mrs Elkins! I believe I would consider what I have to say very seriously, Mrs Elkins. Very seriously. I don't think you want to settle this matter in court, do you?' He smiled meanly.

Josh was getting ready to give Benedict Crowley a kick in the skins. 'No, Josh, there are better ways to cook Mr Crowley's goose.' Elizabeth smiled meanly back.

'Oho, Mrs Elkins,' chortled Mr Crowley. 'I retain some of the best legal minds in the north-east. I don't believe you want to take me on. Benedict Crowley gets what he wants. I have offered to buy your property and am prepared to up the ante to above your asking price. Above, do you hear me, Mrs Elkins? You will find yourself in much legal hot water, believe me, Mrs Elkins, if you do not sell to me.'

'It may interest you to know, Mr Crowley, that I happened to see what you do with property you buy. I was in New Hampshire last weekend and saw your mall and condos. I don't believe you have any intention of keeping this property as it is, as you told me. You misrepresented yourself and your intentions, Mr Crowley.'

'I am a legal buyer,' Crowley grumped. 'Legal buyers can do as they please with the property they purchase. You won't like meeting me in court, Mrs Elkins!'

'On the contrary, I would enjoy seeing you in court, Mr Crowley. I can and will counter-sue you for misrepresentation. And it may interest you to know that I do know something about the law. It's my subject, Mr Crowley. There's nothing I like better than a good old-fashioned courtroom battle . . . especially when I know I've got the strongest case!'

Benedict Crowley turned and stepped off the stoop. 'Just my luck to run into a bloomin' lady lawyer,' he muttered. Without looking back he roared out of the yard in his sleek, overpowered car.

'Good riddance.' Elizabeth wiped her hands gleefully.

'You should have let me sock him one, Mom.'

'No, Josh. Bodily damage is not the way to go. It gets you in a heap of trouble, even if the other guy deserves it. You get the better of a person like Benedict Crowley by out-thinking them. Brain power is the way to go.'

'You really socked it to him, huh, Mom?'

'Yes, I did,' she said proudly. 'He deserved it!'

She waited until the children went out to play to call her parents and tell them the news.

'Hi, Mom, you'll never guess what!'

'You've decided to stay in Vermont,' said her mother without a moment's hesitation.

'Mother, how could you know that?'

'Mothers are not deaf, dumb and blind, dear.'

'But . . . but . . . but I didn't even know it myself. How could you know?'

'Mothers know the direction the wind's blowing, Elizabeth. I'm so happy for you!'

'But . . . thank you,' Elizabeth said humbly.

'I just took a few clues, glued them together, then took the whole thought to its logical conclusion, that's all,' her mother went on. 'Where do

159

you suppose you got your fine legal mind, dear? You didn't pick it off an apple-tree, my darling daughter.'

'Mother,' laughed Elizabeth, 'are you sure you don't want to come up here and go to law school with me?'

'In my next lifetime,' her mother answered. 'For this lifetime I'm very satisfied to see you and the children in a happy situation. Now, you are going to marry Gare, aren't you?'

'Mother!' shrieked Elizabeth.

'Well?' asked her mother, quite unmoved by her daughter's outburst.

'I give up. I really do. I give up.' Elizabeth sighed. 'I should just let my family make all my life's decisions for me.'

'Well, it would be easier,' her mother chuckled. 'Elizabeth, you're a bright young woman. You're also very stubborn, which can be good and bad. Gare is a bright young man. You're admirably well suited to each other. Just let nature take its course. Don't kick and scream all the way. Enjoy yourself. Enjoy being young and having options. Your father and I want most of all for you to be happy. We love you very much, dear.'

'Thank you, Mother. I love you both too. But promise me one thing?'

'What's that, dear?'

'You'll wait until you're invited before you come to our wedding.'

'All right,' her mother laughed. 'I think we can

manage to keep that promise.'

Less than a month later Gare and Elizabeth invited all their friends and relatives to celebrate their marriage in Uncle Abner's yard under the ancient maple-trees.

'This is our wedding-day, our wedding-day, our wedding-day,' Trudy skipped around the kitchen in nervous anticipation.

'It's Mom's and Gare's wedding-day,' Josh corrected her.

'But we belong to Mommy and Mommy is marrying Gare. We go with Mommy,' the little girl explained. 'So that means we are marrying Gare too!'

'Oh brother,' Josh rolled his eyes.

The minister was halfway through the marriage service, when there was a stir in the crowd. People side-stepped and tittered. Up to the bride and groom waddled a bigger and fatter Coonish. 'Burr . . . chit,' he churred.

'Oh my,' laughed Elizabeth.

The no-longer-little coon stood up on his back legs and begged Gare to pick him up.

'Coonish wants to be part of the wedding too,' Trudy said.

'Can he?' asked Josh.

Gare and Elizabeth looked at each other and burst into laughter. 'If it's all right with Rev. Wheeler,' Elizabeth answered.

Rev. Wheeler pushed his glasses back up his nose. 'This is highly unusual,' he grinned. 'A first for me, I must say . . . but, I have no objections.'

So the service was completed with Trudy holding Elizabeth's hand, Elizabeth holding Gare's free hand, Gare holding Coonish and Joshua looking mighty proud with his hands in his pockets.

They sat for their wedding portrait with the children and the coon, and because Trudy thought it only fair — Reina the duck. They laughed and they danced and couldn't believe that so much happiness had come into their lives. 'I love you, Gare Stannard.'

'And I you, Cassie Elizabeth.'

Later, as they left for their honeymoon, Elizabeth remembered to tell Gare about Benedict Crowley appearing on her doorstep.

'Hurrah for my wife, I couldn't have done it better,' he cheered.

'No?' she asked.

'Well . . . maybe . . .'

'Well? Maybe?' she questioned.

'No well or maybe about it,' he grinned. 'I couldn't have done it half so well.' He laughed. 'Look out for my wife. She's definitely a lady who knows what she wants!'